I0654684

Mrs. Hannah Cowley

The Belle's Stratagem

A comedy, as acted at the Theatre-Royal in Covent-Garden

Mrs. Hannah Cowley

The Belle's Stratagem
A comedy, as acted at the Theatre-Royal in Covent-Garden

ISBN/EAN: 9783337184483

Printed in Europe, USA, Canada, Australia, Japan

Cover: Foto ©Andreas Hilbeck / pixelio.de

More available books at **www.hansebooks.com**

THE

BELLE'S STRATAGEM,

A

COMEDY,

AS ACTED AT THE

THEATRE-ROYAL

IN

COVENT-GARDEN.

By Mrs. COWLEY.

LONDON:

Printed for T. CADELL, in the *Strand.*
1782.

THE QUEEN.

MADAM,

IN the following Comedy, my purpofe was, to draw a FEMALE CHARACTER, which with the moft lively Senfibility, fine Underftanding, and elegant Accomplifhments, fhould unite that beautiful Referve and Delicacy which, whilft they veil thofe charms, render them ftill more interefting. In delineating fuch a Character, my heart naturally dedicated it to YOUR MAJESTY; and nothing remained, but permiffion to lay it at Your feet. Your Majefty's gracioufly allowing me this high Honour, is the point to which my hopes afpired, and a reward, of which without cenfure I may be proud.

MADAM,

With the warmeft wifhes for the continuance of your Majefty's felicity,

I am

YOUR MAJESTY's

Moft devoted

and moft dutiful Servant,

H. Cowley.

DRAMATIS PERSONÆ.

M E N.

DORICOURT,	Mr. *Lewis.*
HARDY,	Mr. *Quick.*
SIR GEORGE TOUCHWOOD,	Mr. *Wroughton.*
FLUTTER,	Mr. *Lee Lewes.*
SAVILLE,	Mr. *Aickin.*
VILLERS,	Mr. *Whitfield.*
COURTALL,	Mr. *Robfon.*
SILVERTONGUE,	Mr. *W. Bates.*
CROWQUILL,	Mr. *Jones.*
FIRST GENTLEMAN,	Mr. *Thompfon.*
SECOND GENTLEMAN,	Mr. *L'Eftrange.*
MOUNTEBANK,	Mr. *Booth.*
FRENCH SERVANT,	Mr. *Wewitzer.*
PORTER,	Mr. *Fearon.*
DICK,	Mr. *Stevens.*

W O M E N.

LETITIA HARDY,	Mifs *Younge.*
MRS. RACKET,	Mrs. *Mattocks.*
LADY FRANCES TOUCHWOOD,	Mrs. *Hartley.*
MISS OGLE,	Mrs. *Morton.*
KITTY WILLIS,	Mifs *Stewart.*
LADY,	Mrs. *Pouffin.*

MASQUERADERS, TRADESMEN, SERVANTS, &c.

THE
BELLE'S STRATAGEM.

ACT I.

SCENE I.—*Lincoln's-Inn.*

Enter Saville, *followed by a Servant, at the top of the stage, looking round, as if at a loss.*

Saville.

LINCOLN's-INN!—Well, but where to find him, now I am in Lincoln's-Inn?—Where did he say his Master was?

Serv. He only said in Lincoln's-Inn, Sir.

Sav. That's pretty! And your wisdom never enquired at whose chambers?

Serv. Sir, you spoke to the servant yourself.

Sav. If I was too impatient to ask questions, you ought to have taken directions, blockhead!

Enter Courtall *singing.*

Ha, Courtall!—Bid him keep the horses in motion, and then enquire at all the chambers round.

[*Exit servant.*

What the devil brings you to this part of the town?—Have any of the Long Robes, handsome wives, sisters or chambermaids?

Court. Perhaps they have;—but I came on a different errand; and, had thy good fortune brought thee here half

B   an

an hour fooner, I'd have given thee fuch a treat, ha! ha! ha!

Sav. I'm forry I mifs'd it : what was it ?

Court. I was informed a few days fince, that my coufins Fallow were come to town, and defired earneftly to fee me at their lodgings in Warwick-Court, Holborn. Away drove I, painting them all the way as fo many Hebes. They came from the fartheft part of Northumberland, had never been in town, and in courfe were made up of rufticity, innocence, and beauty.

Sav. Well !

Court. After waiting thirty minutes, during which there was a violent buftle, in bounced five fallow damfels, four of them maypoles ;—the fifth, Nature, by way of variety, had bent in the Æfop ftyle.—But they all opened at once, like hounds on a frefh fcent :—" Oh, " coufin Courtall !—How do you do, coufin Courtall ! " Lord, coufin, I am glad you are come ! We want you " to go with us to the Park, and the Plays, and the " Opera, and Almack's, and all the fine places !"—— The devil, thought I, my dears, may attend you, for I am fure I won't.—However, I heroically ftayed an hour with them, and difcovered, the virgins were all come to town with the hopes of leaving it—Wives :—their heads full of Knight-Baronights, Fops, and adventures.

Sav. Well, how did you get off?

Court. Oh, pleaded a million engagements.——However, confcience twitched me ; fo I breakfafted with them this morning, and afterwards 'fquired them to the gardens here, as the moft private place in town ; and then took a forrowful leave, complaining of my hard, hard fortune, that obliged me to fet off immediately for Dorfetfhire, ha ! ha ! ha !

Sav. I congratulate your efcape !—Courtall at Almack's, with five aukward country coufins ! ha ! ha ! ha !—Why, your exiftence, as a Man of Gallantry, could never have furvived it.   *Court.*

Court. Death, and fire! had they come to town, like the ruftics of the laft age, to fee Paul's, the Lions, and the Wax-work—at their fervice ;—but the coufins of our days come up Ladies—and, with the knowledge they glean from magazines and pocket-books, Fine Ladies ; laugh at the bafhfulnefs of their grandmothers, and boldly demand their *entrées* in the firft circles.

Sav. Where can this fellow be !—Come, give me fome news—I have been at war with woodcocks and partridges thefe two months, and am a ftranger to all that has paffed out of their region.

Court. Oh! enough for three Gazettes. The Ladies are going to petition for a bill, that, during the war, every man may be allowed Two Wives.

Sav. 'Tis impoffible they fhould fucceed, for the majority of both Houfes know what it is to have one.

Court. Gallantry was black-ball'd at the *Coterie* laft Thurfday, and Prudence and Chaftity voted in.

Sav. Ay, that may hold 'till the Camps break up.— But have ye no elopements? no divorces?

Court. Divorces are abfolutely out, and the Commons-Doctors ftarving ; fo they are publifhing trials of *Crim. Con.* with all the feparate evidences at large; which they find has always a wonderful effect on their trade, actions tumbling in upon them afterwards, like mackarel at Gravefend.

Sav. What more?

Court. Nothing—for weddings, deaths, and politics, I never talk of, but whilft my hair is dreffing. But prithee, Saville, how came you in town, whilft all the qualified gentry are playing at pop-gun on Coxheath, and the country over-run with hares and foxes?

Sav. I came to meet my friend Doricourt, who, you know, is lately arrived from Rome.

Court. Arrived! Yes, faith, and has cut us all out! —His carriage, his liveries, his drefs, himfelf, are the

rage

rage of the day! His firſt appearance ſet the whole *Ton* in a ferment, and his valet is beſieged by *levées* of tay-lors, habit-makers, and other Miniſters of Faſhion, to gratify the impatience of their cuſtomers for becoming *à la mode de Doricourt.* Nay, the beautiful Lady Fro-lic, t'other night, with two ſiſter Counteſſes, inſiſted upon his waiſtcoat for muffs; and their ſnowy arms now bear it in triumph about town, to the heart-rending af-fliction of all our *Beaux Garçons.*

Sav. Indeed! Well, thoſe little gallantries will ſoon be over; he's on the point of márriage.

Court. Marriage! Doricourt on the point of marriage! 'Tis the happieſt tidings you could have given, next to his being hanged—Who is the Bride elect?

Sav. I never ſaw her; but 'tis Miſs Hardy, the rich heireſs—the match was made by the parents, and the courtſhip begun on their nurſes knees; Maſter uſed to crow at Miſs, and Miſs uſed to chuckle at Maſter.

Court. Oh! then by this time they care no more for each other, than I do for my country couſins.

Sav. I don't know that; they have never met ſince thus high, and ſo, probably, have ſome regard for each other.

Court. Never met! Odd!

Sav. A whim of Mr. Hardy's; he thought his daugh-ter's charms would make a more forcible impreſſion, if her lover remained in ignorance of them 'till his return from the Continent.

Enter Saville's *Servant.*

Serv. Mr. Doricourt, Sir, has been at Counſellor Pleadwell's, and gone about five minutes.

[*Exit Servant.*

Serv. Five minutes! Zounds! I have been five minutes too late all my life-time!—Good morrow, Courtall; I muſt purſue him. *(Going.)*

Court.

Court. Promife to dine with me to-day; I have fome honeft fellows. *(Going off on the oppofite fide.)*

Sav. Can't promife; perhaps I may.—See there, there's a bevy of female Patagonians, coming down upon us.

Court. By the Lord, then, it muft be my ftrapping coufins.—I dare not look behind me—Run, man, run.

[*Exit, on the fame fide.*

SCENE II.—*A Hall at* Doricourt's. *(A gentle knock at the door.)*

, *Enter the Porter.*

Port. Tap! What fneaking devil art thou? *(Opens the door.)*.

Enter Crowquill.

So! I fuppofe *you* are one of Monfieur's cuftomers too? He's above ftairs, now, overhauling all his Honour's things to a parcel of 'em.

Crowq. No, Sir; it is with you, if you pleafe, that I want to fpeak.

Port. Me! Well, what do you want with me?

Crowq. Sir, you muft know that I am—I am the Gentleman who writes the *Tête-à-têtes* in the Magazines.

Port. Oh, oh!—What, you are the fellow that ties folks together, in your fixpenny cuts, that never meet any where elfe?

Crowq. Oh, dear Sir, excufe me!—we always go on *foundation*; and if you can help me to a few anecdotes of your mafter, fuch as what Marchionefs he loft money to, in Paris—who is his favourite Lady in town—or the name of the Girl he firft made love to at College—or any incidents that happened to his Grandmother, or Great aunts—a couple will do, by way of fupporters—I'll weave a web of intrigues, loffes, and gallantries, between them, that fhall fill four pages, procure me a dozen dinners, and you, Sir, a bottle of wine for your trouble.

Port. Oh, oh! I heard the butler talk of you, when
I lived

I lived at Lord Tinket's. But what the devil do you mean by a bottle of wine! — You gave him a crown for a retaining fee.

Crowq. Oh, Sir, that was for a Lord's amours ; a Commoner's are never but half. Why, I have had a Baronet's for five fhillings, though he was a married man, and changed his miſtreſs every ſix weeks.

Port. Don't tell me! What ſignifies a Baronet, or a bit of a Lord, who, may be, was never further than fun and fun round London ? *We* have travelled, man! My maſter has been in Italy, and over the whole iſland of Spain ; talked to the Queen of France, and danced with her at a maſquerade. Ay, and ſuch folks don't go to maſquerades for nothing ; but mum—not a word more—Unleſs you'll rank my maſter with a Lord, I'll not be guilty of blabbing his ſecrets, I aſſure you.

Crowq. Well, Sir, perhaps you'll throw in a hint or two of other families, where you've lived, that may be worked up into ſomething ; and ſo, Sir, here is one, two, three, four, five ſhillings.

Port. Well, that's honeſt, *(pocketing the money.)* To tell you the truth, I don't know much of my maſter's concerns yet ;—but here comes Monſieur and his gang : I'll pump them : they have trotted after him all round Europe, from the Canaries to the Iſle of Wight.

Enter ſeveral foreign Servants and two Tradeſmen.
(The Porter takes one of them aſide.)

Tradeſm. Well then, you have ſhew'd us all ?

Frenchm. All, *en vérité, Meſſieurs !* you avez ſeen every ting. *Serviteur, ſerviteur.*   [*Exeunt* Tradeſmen.

Ah, here comes one *autre* curious Engliſhman, and dat's one *autre* guinea *pour moi.*

Enter Saville.

Allons, Monſieur, dis way ; I will ſhew you tings, ſuch tings you never ſee, begar, in England !—velvets by Le
Moſſe,

Mosse, suits cut by Verdue, trimmings by Grossette, em-
broidery by Detanville——

Sav. Puppy!—where is your Master?

Port. Zounds! you chattering frog-eating dunder-
head, can't you see a Gentleman?—'Tis Mr. Saville.

Frenchm. Monsieur Saville! *Je suis mort de peur.* —
Ten tousand pardons! *Excusez mon erreur,* and permit
me you conduct to Monsieur Doricourt; he be too happy
à vous voir.   [*Exeunt* Frenchman *and* Saville.

Port. Step below a bit;—we'll make it out some-how!
—I suppose a slice of sirloin won't make the story go down
the worse.   [*Exeunt* Porter *and* Crowquill.

SCENE III.——*An Apartment at* Doricourt's.

Enter Doricourt.

Doric. (*speaking to a servant behind*) I shall be too late
for St. James's; bid him come immediately.

Enter Frenchman *and* Saville.

Frenchm. Monsieur Saville.   [*Exit* Frenchman.

Doric. Most fortunate! My dear Saville, let the warmth
of this embrace speak the pleasure of my heart.

Sav. Well, this is some comfort, after the scurvy re-
ception I met with in your hall.—I prepared my mind, as
I came up stairs, for a *bon jour,* a grimace, and an *adieu.*

Doric. Why so?

Sav. Judging of the master from the rest of the family.
What the devil is the meaning of that flock of foreigners
below, with their parchment faces and snuffy whiskers?
What! can't an Englishman stand behind your carriage,
buckle your shoe, or brush your coat?

Doric. Stale, my dear Saville, stale! Englishmen make
the best Soldiers, Citizens, Artizans, and Philosophers in
the world; but the very worst Footmen. I keep French

· fellows

fellows and Germans, as the Romans kept flaves; becaufe their own countrymen had minds too enlarged and
haughty to defcend with a grace to the duties of fuch a
ftation.

Sav. A good excufe for a bad practice.

Doric. On my honour, experience will convince you
of its truth. A Frenchman neither hears, fees, nor
breathes, but as his mafter directs; and his whole fyftem
of conduct is compris'd in one fhort word, *Obedience!*
An Englifhman reafons, forms opinions, cogitates, and
difputes; he is the mere creature of your will: the other,
a being, confcious of equal importance in the univerfal
fcale with yourfelf, and is therefore your judge, whilft
he wears your livery, and decides on your actions with
the freedom of a cenfor.

Sav. And this in defence of a cuftom I have heard
you execrate, together with all the adventitious manners
imported by our Travell'd Gentry.

Doric. Ay, but that was at eighteen; we are always *very*
wife at eighteen. But confider this point: we go into
Italy, where the fole bufinefs of the people is to ftudy and
improve the powers of Mufic: we yield to the fafcination,
and grow enthufiafts in the charming fcience: we travel
over France, and fee the whole kingdom compofing or-
naments, and inventing Fafhions: we condefcend to avail
ourfelves of their induftry, and adopt their modes: we
return to England, and find the nation intent on the moft
important objects; Polity, Commerce, War, with all the
Liberal Arts, employ her fons; the latent fparks glow afrefh
within our bofoms; the fweet follies of the Continent im-
perceptibly flide away, whilft Senators, Statefmen, Patriots and Heroes, emerge from the *virtù* of Italy, and the
frippery of France.

Sav. I may as well give it up! You had always the
art of placing your faults in the beft light; and I can't
help

help loving you, faults and all: fo, to ftart a fubject which muft pleafe you, When do you expect Mifs Hardy?

Doric. Oh, the hour of expectation is paft. She is arrived, and I this morning had the honour of an interview at Pleadwell's. The writings were ready; and, in obedience to the will of Mr. Hardy, we met to fign and feal.

Sav. Has the event anfwered? Did your heart leap, or fink, when you beheld your Miftrefs?

Doric. Faith, neither one nor t'other; fhes a fine girl, as far as mere flefh and blood goes. ——But——

Sav. But what?

Doric. Why, fhe's *only* a fine girl; complexion, fhape, and features; nothing more.

Sav. Is not that enough?

Doric. No! fhe fhould have fpirit! fire! *l'air enjoué!* that fomething, that nothing, which every body feels, and which no body can defcribe, in the refiftlefs charmers of Italy and France.

Sav. Thanks to the parfimony of my father, that kept me from travel! I would not have loft my relifh for true unaffected Englifh beauty, to have been quarrell'd for by all the Belles of Verfailles and Florence.

Doric. Pho! thou haft no tafte. *Englifh* beauty! 'Tis infipidity; it wants the zeft, it wants poignancy, Frank! Why, I have known a Frenchwoman, indebted to nature for no one thing but a pair of decent eyes, reckon in her fuite as many Counts, Marquiffes, and *Petits Maîtres*, as would fatisfy three dozen of our firft-rate toafts. I have known an Italian *Marquizina* make ten conquefts in ftepping from her carriage, and carry her flaves from one city to another, whofe real intrinfic beauty would have yielded to half the little *Grifettes* that pace your Mall on a Sunday.

Sav. And has Mifs Hardy nothing of this?

Doric. If fhe has, fhe was pleafed to keep it to herfelf. I was in the room half an hour before I could catch the

C colour

colour of her eyes; and every attempt to draw her into conversation occasioned so cruel an embarrassment, that I was reduced to the necessity of news, French fleets, and Spanish captures, with her father.

Sav. So Miss Hardy, with only beauty, modesty, and merit, is doom'd to the arms of a husband who will despise her.

Doric. You are unjust. Though she has not inspir'd me with violent passion, my honour secures her felicity.

Sav. Come, come, Doricourt, you know very well that when the honour of a husband is *locum-tenens* for his heart, his wife must be as indifferent as himself, if she is not unhappy.

Doric. Pho! never moralise without spectacles. But, as we are upon the tender subject, how did you bear Touch-wood's carrying Lady Frances?

Sav. You know I never look'd up to her with hope, and Sir George is every way worthy of her.

Doric. *A la mode Angloise*, a philosopher even in love.

Sav. Come, I detain you—you seem dress'd at all points, and of course have an engagement.

Doric. To St. James's. I dine at Hardy's, and accompany them to the masquerade in the evening: but break-fast with me to-morrow, and we'll talk of our old companions; for I swear to you, Saville, the air of the Continent has not effaced one youthful prejudice or attachment.

Sav. —With an exception to the case of Ladies and Servants.

Doric. True; there I plead guilty:—but I have never yet found any man whom I could cordially take to my heart, and call Friend, who was not born beneath a British sky, and whose heart and manners were not truly English.

[*Ex.* Doricourt *and* Saville.

SCENE

SCENE IV.—*An Apartment at Mr.* Hardy's.
Villers *feated on a fopha; reading.*

Enter Flutter.

Flut. Hah, Villers, have you feen Mrs. Racket ?——
Mifs Hardy, I find, is out.

Vill. I have not feen her yet. I have made a voyage to
Lapland fince I came in. *(flinging away the book.)* A
Lady at her toilette is as difficult to be moved, as a Qua-
ker, *(yawning).* What events have happened in the world
fince yefterday ? have you heard ?

Flut. Oh, yes; I ftopt at Tatterfall's as I came by,
and there I found Lord James Jeffamy, Sir William
Wilding, and Mr. ———. But, now I think of it, you
fha'n't know a fyllable of the matter ; for I have been
informed you never believe above one half of what I fay.

Vill. My dear fellow, fomebody has impofed upon you
moft egregioufly !—Half ! Why, I never believe one tenth
part of what you fay ; that is, according to the plain and
literal expreffion : but, as I underftand you, your intelligence is amufing.

Flut. That's very hard now, very hard. I never re-
lated a falfity in my life, unlefs I ftumbled on it by miftake ; and if it were otherwife, your dull matter-of-fact
people are infinitely oblig'd to thofe warm imaginations
which foar into fiction to amufe you; for, pofitively, the
common events of this little dirty world are not worth
talking about, unlefs you embellifh 'em !——Hah ! here
comes Mrs. Rackett : Adieu to weeds, I fee ! All life!

Enter Mrs. Rackett.

Enter, Madam, in all your charms ! Villers has been abu-
fing your toilette for keeping you fo long ; but I think
we are much oblig'd to it, and fo are you.

Mrs. *Rack.* How fo, pray ? Good-morning t'ye both.
Here, here's a hand a-piece for you. *(They kifs her hands.)*

Flut. How fo ! Becaufe it has given you fo many
beauties.

Mrs.

Mrs. Rack. Delightful compliment ! What do you think of that, Villers ?

· *Vill.* That he and his compliments are alike—fhewy, but won't bear examining .——So you brought Mifs Hardy to town laft night ?

Mrs. Rack. Yes, I fhould have brought her before, but I had a fall from my horfe, that confined me a week. —I fuppofe in her heart fhe wifhed me hanged a dozen times an hour.

Flut. Why ?

Mrs. Rack. Had fhe not an expecting Lover in town all the time ? She meets him this morning at the Lawyer's. —I hope fhe'll charm him ; fhe's the fweeteft girl in the world.

Vill. Vanity, like murder, will out.—You have convinced me you think yourfelf more charming.

Mrs. Rack. How can that be ?

Vill. No woman ever praifes another, unlefs fhe thinks herfelf fuperior in the very perfections fhe allows.

Flut. Nor no man ever rails at the fex, unlefs he is confcious he deferves their hatred.

Mrs. Rack. Thank ye, Flutter—I'll owe ye a *bouquet* for that. I am going to vifit the new-married Lady Frances Touchwood.—Who knows her hufband ?

Flut. Every body.

Mrs. Rack. Is there not fomething odd in his character ?

Vill. Nothing, but that he is paffionately fond of his wife ;—and fo petulant is his love, that he open'd the cage of a favourite Bullfinch, and fent it to catch Butterflies, becaufe fhe rewarded its fong with her kiffes.

Mrs. Rack. Intolerable monfter ! Such a brute deferves————

Vill. Nay, nay, nay, nay, this is your fex now —— Give a woman but one ftroke of character, off fhe goes, like a ball from a racket ; fees the whole man, marks

him

him down for an angel or a devil, and fo exhibits him
to her acquaintance.—This monfter! this brute! is one
of the worthieft fellows upon earth; found fenfe, and· a
liberal mind ; but doats on his wife to fuch excefs, that
he quarrels with every thing fhe admires, and is jealous
of her tippet and nofegay.

Mrs. *Rack.* Oh, lefs love for me, kind Cupid! I can
fee no difference between the torment of fuch an affection, and hatred.

Flut. Oh, pardon me, inconceivable difference, inconceivable ; I fee it as clearly as your bracelet.   In the one
cafe the hufband would fay, as Mr. Snapper faid t'other
day, Zounds! Madam, do you fuppofe that *my* table, and
my houfe, and *my* pictures!—*A-propos, des Bottes.*   There
was the divineft Plague of Athens fold yefterday at Lang-
ford's! the dead figures fo natural, you would have fworn
they had been alive!   Lord Primrofe bid Five hundred—
Six, faid Lady Carmine.—A thoufand, faid Ingot the Na-
bob.—Down went the hammer.—A *rouleau* for your bargain, faid Sir Jeremy Jingle.   And what anfwer do you
think Ingot made him ?

Mrs. *Racket.* Why, took the offer.

Flut. Sir, I would oblige you, but I buy this picture
to place in the nurfery : the children have already got
Whittington and his Cat ; 'tis juft this fize, and they'll
make good companions.

Mrs. *Rack.* Ha! ha! ha! Well, I proteft that's juft
the way now—the Nabobs and their wives outbid one at
every fale, and the creatures have no more tafte——

Vill. There again ! You forget this ftory is told by
Flutter, who always remembers every thing but the
circumftances and the perfon he talks about : — 'twas
Ingot who offer'd a *rouleau* for the bargain, and Sir
Jeremy Jingle who made the reply.

Flut. Egad, I believe you are right. — Well, the ftory
is as good one way as t'other, you know. Good morning.
I am

I am going to Mrs. Crotchet's concert, and in my way back shall make my bow at Sir George's. *(Going)*

Vill. I'll venture every figure in your taylor's bill, you make some blunder there.

Flut. (turning back) Done! My taylor's bill has not been paid these two years; and I'll open my mouth with as much care as Mrs. Bridget Button, who wears cork plumpers in each cheek, and never hazards more than six words for fear of shewing them.   [*Exit* Flutter.

Mrs. Rack. 'Tis a good-natur'd insignificant creature! let in every where, and cared for no where.—There's Miss Hardy return'd from Lincoln's-Inn:—she seems rather chagrin'd.

Vill. Then I leave you to your communications.

Enter Letitia, *followed by her Maid.*

Adieu! I am rejoiced to see you so well, Madam! but I must tear myself away.

Letit. Don't vanish in a moment.

Vill. Oh, inhuman! you are two of the most dangerous women in town—Staying here to be cannonaded by four such eyes, is equal to a *rencontre* with Paul Jones, or a midnight march to Omoa!—They'll swallow the nonsense for the sake of the compliment. *(Aside)*
                                                    [*Exit* Villers.

Letit. (gives her cloak to her maid.) Order Du Quesne never to come again; he shall positively dress my hair no more. [*Exit Maid.*]   And this odious silk, how unbecoming it is!—I was bewitched to chuse it. *(Throwing herself on a sopha, and looking in a pocket-glass, Mrs. Racket staring at her.)* Did you ever see such a fright as I am to-day?

Mrs. Rack. Yes, I have seen you look much worse.

Letit. How can you be so provoking? If I do not look this morning worse than ever I look'd in my life, I am naturally a fright. You shall have it which way you will.
                                                    .. Mrs.

Mrs. *Rack*. Juſt as you pleaſe ; but pray what is the meaning of all this ?

Letit. *(riſing.)* Men are all diſſemblers ! flatterers ! deceivers ! Have I not heard a thouſand times of my air, my eyes, my ſhape — all made for victory ! and to-day, when I bent my whole heart on one poor conqueſt, I have proved that all thoſe imputed charms amount to no-thing ;—for Doricourt ſaw them unmov'd.—A huſband of fifteen months could not have examin'd me with more cutting indifference.

Mrs. *Rack*. Then you return it like a wife of fifteen months, and be as indifferent as he.

Letit. Aye, there's the ſting ! The blooming boy, who left his image in my young heart, is at four and twenty improv'd in every grace that fix'd him there. It is the ſame face that my memory, and my dreams, con-ſtantly painted to me ; but its graces are finiſhed, and every beauty heightened. How mortifying, to feel my-ſelf at the ſame moment his ſlave, and an object of per-fect indifference to him !

Mrs. *Rack*. How are you certain that was the caſe ? Did you expect him to kneel down before the lawyer, his clerks, and your father, to make oath of your beauty ?

Letit. No ; but he ſhould have look'd as if a ſudden ray had pierced him ! he ſhould have been breathleſs ! ſpeechleſs ! for, oh ! Caroline, all this was I.

Mrs. *Rack*. I am ſorry you was ſuch a fool. Can you expect a man, who has courted and been courted by half the fine women in Europe, to feel like a girl from a boarding-ſchool ? He is the prettieſt fellow you have ſeen, and in courſe bewilders your imagination ; but he has ſeen a million of pretty women, child, before he ſaw you ; and his firſt feelings have been over long ago.

Letit. Your raillery diſtreſſes me ; but I will touch his heart, or never be his wife.

Mrs. Rack. Abfurd, and romantic! If you have no reafon to believe his heart pre-engaged, be fatisfied; if he is a man of honour, you'll have nothing to complain of.

Letit. Nothing to complain of! Heav'ns! fhall I marry the man I adore, with fuch an expectation as that?

Mrs. Rack. And when you have fretted yourfelf pale, my dear, you'll have mended your expectation greatly.

Letit. (paufing.) Yet I have one hope. If there is any power whofe peculiar care is faithful love, that power I invoke to aid me.

Enter Mr. Hardy.

Hardy. Well, now; wasn't I right? Aye, Letty! Aye, Coufin Racket! wasn't I right? I knew 'twould be fo. He was all agog to fee her before he went abroad; and, if he had, he'd have thought no more of her face, may be, than his own.

Mrs. Rack. May be, not half fo much.

Hardy. Aye, may be fo:—but I fee into things; exactly as I forefaw, to-day he fell defperately in love with the wench, he! he! he!

Letit. Indeed, Sir! how did you perceive it?

Hardy. That's a pretty queftion! How do I perceive every thing? How did I forefee the fall of corn, and the rife of taxes? How did I know, that if we quarrelled with America, Norway deals would be dearer? How did I foretell that a war would fink the funds? How did I forewarn Parfon Homily, that if he didn't fome way or other contrive to get more votes than Rubrick, he'd lofe the lecturefhip? How did I——But what the devil makes you fo dull, Letitia? I thought to have found you popping about as brifk as the jacks of your harpfichord.

Letit.

Letit. Surely, Sir, 'tis a very ferious occafion.

Hardy. Pho, pho! girls fhould never be grave before marriage. How did you feel, Coufin, beforehand? Aye!

Mrs. Rack. Feel! why exceedingly full of cares.

Hardy. Did you?

Mrs. Rack. I could not fleep for thinking of my coach, my liveries, and my chairmen; the tafte of clothes I fhould be prefented in, diftracted me for a week; and whether I fhould be married in white or lilac, gave me the moft cruel anxiety.

Letit. And is it poffible that you felt no other care?

Hardy. And pray, of what fort may your cares be, Mrs. Letitia? I begin to forefee now that you have taken a diflike to Doricourt.

Letit. Indeed, Sir, I have not.

Hardy. Then what's all this melancholy about? A'n't you going to be married? and, what's more, to a fenfible man? and, what's more to a young girl, to a handfome man? And what's all this melancholy for, I fay?

Mrs. Rack. Why, becaufe he *is* handfome and fenfible, and becaufe fne's over head and ears in love with him; all which, it feems, your foreknowledge had not told you a word of.

Letit. Fye, Caroline!

Hardy. Well, come, do you tell me what's the matter then? If you don't like him, hang the figning and fealing, he fha'n't have ye:—and yet I can't fay that neither; for you know that eftate, that coft his father and me upwards of fourfcore thoufand pounds, muft go all to him if you won't have him: if he won't have you, indeed, 'twill be all yours. All that's clear, engrofs'd upon parchment, and the poor dear man fet his hand to it whilft he was a dying.—"Ah!" faid I, "I forefee you'll "never live to fee 'em come together; but their firft fon

D   fhall

" ſhall be chriſtened Jeremiah after you, that I promiſe
" you."——But come, I ſay, what is the matter? Don't
you like him?

Letit. I fear, Sir—if I muſt ſpeak—I fear I was leſs
agreeable in Mr. Doricourt's eyes, than he appeared in
mine.

Hardy. There you are miſtaken; for I aſked him,
and he told me he liked you vaſtly. Don't you think he
muſt have taken a fancy to her?

Mrs. Rack. Why really I think ſo, as I was not by.

Letit. My dear Sir, I am convinced he has not; but
if there is ſpirit or invention in woman, he ſhall.

Hardy. Right, Girl; go to your toilette—

Letit. It is not my toilette that can ſerve me: but a
plan has ſtruck me, if you will not oppoſe it, which flat-
ters me with brilliant ſucceſs.

Hardy. Oppoſe it! not I indeed! What is it?

Letit. Why, Sir—it may ſeem a little paradoxical;
but, as he does not like me enough, I want him to like
me ſtill leſs, and will at our next interview endeavour to
heighten his indifference into diſlike.

Hardy. Who the devil could have foreſeen that?

Mrs. Rack. Heaven and earth! Letitia, are you ſerious?

Letit. As ſerious as the moſt important buſineſs of my
life demands.

Mrs. Rack. Why endeavour to make him diſlike
you?

Letit. Becauſe 'tis much eaſier to convert a ſentiment
into its oppoſite, than to transform indifference into
tender paſſion.

Mrs. Rack. That may be good philoſophy, but I am
afraid you'll find it a bad maxim.

Letit. I have the ſtrongeſt confidence in it. I am in-
ſpired with unuſual ſpirits, and on this hazard willingly
ſtake

ftake my chance for happinefs. I am impatient to begin my meafures.   [*Exit* Letitia.

Hardy. Can you forefee the end of this, Coufin?

Mrs. Rack. No, Sir; nothing lefs than your penetration can do that, I am fure; and I can't ftay now to confider it. I am going to call on the Ogles, and then to Lady Frances Touchwood's, and then to an Auction, and then—I don't know where——but I fhall be at home time enough to witnefs this extraordinary interview. Good-bye.   [*Exit Mrs.* Racket.

Hardy. Well, 'tis an odd thing—I can't underftand it—but I forefee Letty will have her way, and fo I fha'n't give myfelf the trouble to difpute it.

[*Exit* Hardy.

END OF THE FIRST ACT.

A C T   II.

SCENE I. *Sir George Touchwood's.*

Enter Doricourt *and* Sir George.

Doricourt.

MARRIED, ha! ha! ha! you, whom I heard in Paris fay fuch things of the fex, are in London a married man.

Sir Geo. The fex is ftill what it has ever been fince *la petite morale* banifhed fubftantial virtues; and rather than have given my name to one of your high-bred fafhionable dames, I'd have croffed the line in a fire-fhip, and married a Japanefe.

Doria

Doric. Yet you have married an English beauty, yea, and a beauty born in high life.

Sir Geo. True; but she has a simplicity of heart and manners, that would have become the fair Hebrew damsels toasted by the Patriarchs.

Doric. Ha! ha! Why, thou art a downright matrimonial Quixote. My life on't, she becomes as mere a Town Lady in six months as though she had been bred to the trade.

Sir Geo. Common—common—(*contemptuously*). No, Sir, Lady Frances despises high life so much from the ideas I have given her, that she'll live in it like a salamander in fire.

Doric. Oh, that the circle *dans la place Victoire* could witness thy extravagance! I'll send thee off to St. Evreux this night, drawn at full length, and coloured after nature.

Sir Geo. Tell him then, to add to the ridicule, that Touchwood glories in the name of Husband; that he has found in one Englishwoman more beauty than Frenchmen ever saw, and more goodness than Frenchwomen can conceive.

Doric. Well—enough of description. Introduce me to this phœnix; I came on purpose.

Sir Geo. Introduce!—oh, aye, to be sure—I believe Lady Frances is engaged just now—but another time. How handsome the dog looks to-day! *Aside.*

Doric. Another time!—but I have no other time. 'Sdeath! this is the only hour I can command this fortnight!

Sir Geo. [*Aside.* I am glad to hear it, with all my soul.] So then, you can't dine with us to-day? That's very unlucky.

Doric. Oh, yes—as to dinner—yes, I can, I believe, contrive to dine with you to-day.

Sir

Sir Geo. Pſha! I didn't think on what I was ſaying;
I meant ſupper—You can't ſup with us?

Doric. Why, ſupper will be rather more convenient
than dinner—But you are fortunate—if you had aſk'd me
any other night, I could not have come.

Sir Geo. To-night!—Gad, now I recollect, we are
particularly engaged to-night.—But to-morrow night—

Doric. Why look ye, Sir George, 'tis very plain you
have no inclination to let me ſee your wife at all; ſo
here I ſit (*throws himſelf on a ſopha.*)—There's my hat,
and here are my legs.—Now I ſha'n't ſtir till I have ſeen
her; and I have no engagements: I'll breakfaſt, dine,
and ſup with you every day this week.

Sir Geo. Was there ever ſuch a provoking wretch!
But, to be plain with you, Doricourt, I and my houſe
are at your ſervice: but you are a damn'd agreeable fellow, and ten years younger than I am; and the women,
I obſerve, always ſimper when you appear. For theſe
reaſons, I had rather, when Lady Frances and I are together, that you ſhould forget we are acquainted, further
than a nod, a ſmile, or a how-d'ye.

Doric. Very well.

Sir Geo. It is not merely yourſelf *in propriâ perſonâ*
that I object to; but, if you are intimate here, you'll
make my houſe ſtill more the faſhion than it is; and it
is already ſo much ſo, that my doors are of no uſe to me.
I married Lady Frances to engroſs her to myſelf; yet ſuch
is the bleſſed freedom of modern manners, that, in ſpite
of me, her eyes, thoughts, and converſation, are conti-
nually divided amongſt all the Flirts and Coxcombs of
Faſhion.

Doric. To be ſure, I confeſs that kind of freedom is
carried rather too far. 'Tis hard one can't have a jewel
in one's cabinet, but the whole town muſt be gratified
with its luſtre. He ſha'n't preach me out of ſeeing his
wife, though. *Aſide.*

Sir

Sir Geo. Well, now, that's reafonable. When you take time to reflect, Doricourt, I always obferve you decide right, and therefore I hope——

Enter Servant.

Serv. Sir, my Lady defires——

Sir Geo. I am particularly engaged.

Doric. Oh, Lord, that fhall be no excufe in the world *(leaping from the fopha)*. Lead the way, John.— I'll attend your Lady.   [*Exit, following the Servant.*

Sir Geo. What devil poffeffed me to talk about her!— Here, Doricourt! *(Running after him.)* Doricourt!

Enter Mrs. Racket, *and* Mifs Ogle, *followed by a Servant.*

Mrs. Rack. Acquaint your Lady, that Mrs. Racket, and Mifs Ogle, are here.   [*Exit* Servant.

Mifs Ogle. I fhall hardly know Lady Frances, 'tis fo long fince I was in Shropfhire.

Mrs. Rack. And I'll be fworn you never faw her *out* of Shropfhire.—Her father kept her locked up with his Caterpillars and Shells ; and loved her beyond any thing —but a blue Butterfly, and a petrified Frog !

Mifs Ogle. Ha! ha! ha!—Well, 'twas a cheap way of breeding her :—you know he was very poor, though a Lord ; and very high-fpirited, though a Virtuofo.— In town, her Pantheons, Operas, and Robes de Cour, would have fwallowed his Sea-Weeds, Moths, and Monfters, in fix weeks !—Sir George, I find, thinks his Wife a moft extraordinary creature : he has taught her to defpife every thing like Fafhionable Life, and boafts that example will have no effect on her.

Mrs. Rack. There's a great degree of impertinence in all that—I'll try to make her a Fine Lady, to humble him.

Mifs Ogle. That's juft the thing I wifh.

Enter

Enter Lady Frances.

Lady Fran. I beg ten thoufand pardons, my dear Mrs. Racket.—Mifs Ogle, I rejoice to fee you : I fhould have come to you fooner, but I was detained in conver⸗ fation by Mr. Doricourt.

Mrs. Rack. Pray make no apology ; I am quite happy that we have your Ladyfhip in town at laft.—What ftay do you make ?

Lady Fran. A fhort one ! Sir George talks with regret of the fcenes we have left ; and as the ceremony of pre⸗ fentation is over, will, I believe, foon return.

Mifs Ogle. Sure he can't be fo cruel ! Does your La⸗ dyfhip wifh to return fo foon ?

Lady Fran. I have not the habit of confulting my own wifhes ; but, I think, if they decide, we fhall not return immediately. I have yet hardly form'd an idea of Lon⸗ don.

Mrs. Rack. I fhall quarrel with your Lord and Mafter, if he dares think of depriving us of you fo foon. How do you difpofe of yourfelf to-day ?

Lady Fran. Sir George is going with me this morning to the mercer's, to chufe a filk ; and then——

Mrs. Rack. Chufe a filk for you ! ha ! ha ! ha ! Sir George chufes your laces too, I hope ; your gloves, and your pincufhions !

Lady Fran. Madam !

Mrs. Rack. I am glad to fee you blufh, my dear Lady Frances. Thefe are ftrange homefpun ways ! If you do thefe things, pray keep 'em fecret. Lord blefs us ! If the Town fhould know your hufband chufes your gowns !

Mifs Ogle. You are very young, my Lady, and have been brought up in folitude. The maxims you learnt among the Wood-Nymphs in Shropfhire, won't pafs current here, I affure you.

Mrs. Rack. Why, my dear creature, you look quite frighten'd !—Come, you fhall go with us to an Exhibi-

tion,

tion, and an Auction.—Afterwards, we'll take a turn in the Park, and then drive to Kensington ;—so we shall be at home by four, to dress; and in the evening I'll attend you to Lady Brilliant's masquerade.

Lady Fran. I shall be very happy to be of your party, if Sir George has no engagements.

Mrs. Rack. What ! Do you stand so low in your own opinion, that you dare not trust yourself without Sir George ! If you chuse to play Darby and Joan, my dear, you should have stay'd in the country ;—'tis an Exhibition not calculated for London, I assure you !

Miss Ogle. What I suppose, my Lady, you and Sir George, will be seen pacing it comfortably round the Canal, arm and arm, and then go lovingly into the same carriage ;—dine *tête-à-tête*, spend the evening at Picquet, and so go soberly to bed at Eleven !—Such a snug plan may do for an Attorney and his Wife ; but, for Lady Frances Touchwood, 'tis as unsuitable as linsey-woolfey, or a black bonnet at the *Festino !*

Lady Fran. These are rather new doctrines to me !—But, my dear Mrs. Rackett, you and Miss Ogle must judge of these things better than I can. As you observe, I am but young, and may have caught absurd opinions.—Here is Sir George !

Enter Sir George.

Sir Geo. (*Aside.*) 'Sdeath ! another room full !

Lady Fran. My love ! Mrs. Racket, and the Miss Ogles.

Mrs. Rack. Give you joy, Sir George.—We came to rob you of Lady Frances for a few hours.

Sir Geo. A few hours !

Lady Fran. Oh, yes ! I am going to an Exhibition, and an Auction, and the Park, and Kensington, and a thousand places !—It is quite ridiculous, I find, for married people to be always together—We shall be laughed at !

Sir

Sir Geo. I am aftonifhed !—Mrs. Racket, what does the dear creature mean ?

Mrs. Rack. Mean, Sir George !—what fhe fays, I imagine.

Mifs Ogle. Why, you know, Sir, as Lady Frances had the misfortune to be bred entirely in the Country, fhe cannot be fuppofed to be verfed in Fafhionable Life.

Sir Geo. No; heaven forbid fhe fhould !—If fhe had, Madam, fhe would never have been my Wife !

Mrs. Rack. Are you ferious ?

Sir Geo. Perfe&ly fo.—I fhould never have had the courage to have married a well-bred Fine Lady.

Mifs Ogle. Pray, Sir, what do you take a Fine Lady to be, that you exprefs fuch fear of her ? *(fneeringly.)*

Sir Geo. A being eafily defcribed, Madam, as fhe is feen every where, but in her own houfe. She fleeps at home, but fhe lives all over the town. In her mind, every fentiment gives place to the Luft of Conqueft, and the vanity of being particular. The feelings of Wife, and Mother, are loft in the whirl of diffipation. If fhe continues virtuous, 'tis by chance—and if fhe preferves her Hufband from ruin, 'tis by her dexterity at the Card-Table !—Such a Woman I take to be a perfe& Fine Lady !

Mrs. Rack. And you I take to be a flanderous Cynic of two-and-thirty.—Twenty years hence, one might have forgiven fuch a libel !—Now, Sir, hear my definition of a Fine Lady :—She is a creature for whom Nature has done much, and Education more ; fhe has Tafte, Elegance, Spirit, Underftanding. In her manner fhe is free, in her morals nice. Her behaviour is undiftinguifhingly polite to her Hufband, and all mankind ;—her fentiments are for their hours of retirement. In a word, a Fine Lady is the life of converfation, the fpirit of fociety, the joy of the public !—Pleafure follows where ever fhe appears, and the kindeft wifhes attend her flumbers,

bers.—Make hafte, then, my dear Lady Frances, com-
mence Fine Lady, and force your Hufband to acknow-
ledge the juftnefs of my picture !

Lady Fran. I am fure 'tis a delightful one. How can
you diflike it, Sir George ? You painted Fafhionable Life
in colours fo difgufting, that I thought I hated it; but,
on a nearer view, it feems charming. I have hitherto
lived in obfcurity; 'tis time that I fhould be a Woman
of the World. I long to begin ;—my heart pants with
expectation and delight !

Mrs. Rack. Come, then ; let us begin directly. I am
impatient to introduce you to that Society, which you
were born to ornament and charm.

Lady Fran. Adieu ! my Love !—We fhall meet again
at dinner. *(Going.)*

Sir Geo. Sure, I am in a dream !—Fanny !

Lady Fran. *(returning)* Sir George ?

Sir Geo. Will you go without me ?

Mrs. Rack. Will you go without me !—ha ! ha ! ha !
what a pathetic addrefs! Why, fure you would not always
be feen fide by fide, like two beans upon a ftalk. Are you
afraid to truft Lady Frances with me, Sir ?

Sir George. Heaven and earth ! with whom can a man
truft his wife, in the prefent ftate of fociety ? Formerly
there were diftinctions of character amongft ye : every
clafs of females had its particular defcription ; Grandmothers were pious, Aunts difcreet, Old Maids cenforious!
but now aunts, grandmothers, girls, and maiden gentlewomen, are all the fame creature ;—a wrinkle more or
lefs is the fole difference between ye.

Mrs. Rack. That Maiden Gentlewomen have loft their
cenforioufnefs, is furely not in your catalogue of grievances.

Sir Geo. Indeed it is—and ranked amongft the moft
ferious grievances.—Things went well, Madam, when the
tongues of three or four old Virgins kept all the Wives

and

and Daughters of a parish in awe. They were the Dragons that guarded the Hesperian fruit; and I wonder they have not been oblig'd, by act of parliament, to resume their function.

Mrs. Rack. Ha! ha! ha! and pension'd, I suppose, for making strict enquiries into the lives and conversations of their neighbours.

Sir Geo. With all my heart, and impowered to oblige every woman to conform her conduct to her real situation. You, for instance, are a Widow: your air should be sedate, your dress grave, your deportment matronly, and in all things an example to the young women growing up about you!—instead of which, you are dress'd for conquest, think of nothing but ensnaring hearts; are a Coquette, a Wit, and a Fine Lady.

Mrs. Rack. Bear witness to what he says! A Coquette! a Wit! and a Fine Lady! Who would have expected an eulogy from such an ill-natur'd mortal!—Valour to a Soldier, Wisdom to a Judge, or glory to a Prince, is not more than such a character to a Woman.

Miss Ogle. Sir George, I see, languishes for the charming society of a century and a half ago; when a grave 'Squire, and a still graver Dame, surrounded by a sober family, form'd a stiff groupe in a mouldy old house in the corner of a Park.

Mrs. Rack. Delightful serenity! Undisturb'd by any noise but the cawing of rooks, and the quarterly rumbling of an old family-coach on a state-visit; with the happy intervention of a friendly call from the Parish Apothecary, or the Curate's Wife.

Sir Geo. And what is the society of which you boast?—a mere chaos, in which all distinction of rank is lost in a ridiculous affectation of ease, and every different order of beings huddled together, as they were before the creation. In the same *select party*, you will often find the wife of a Bishop and a Sharper, of an Earl and a Fidler. In short, 'tis one universal masquerade, all disguised in the same habits and manners. *Serv.*

Serv. Mr. Flutter. | *Exit* Servant.

Sir Geo. Here comes an illuftration. Now I defy you to tell from his appearance, whether Flutter is a Privy Counfellor or a Mercer, a Lawyer, or a Grocer's 'Prentice.

Enter Flutter.

Flut. Oh, juft which you pleafe, Sir George ; fo you don't make me a Lord Mayor. Ah, Mrs. Racket !—— Lady Frances, your moft obedient ; you look—now hang me, if that's not provoking !—had your gown been of another colour, I fhould have faid the prettieft thing you ever heard in your life.

Mifs Ogle. Pray give it us.

Flut. I was yefterday at Mrs. Bloomer's. She was drefs'd all in green ; no other colour to be feen but that of her face and bofom. So fays I, My dear Mrs. Bloomer ! you look like a Carnation, juft burfting from its pod.

Sir Geo. And what faid her Hufband ?

Flut. Her Hufband ! Why, her Hufband laugh'd, and faid a Cucumber would have been a happier fimile.

Sir Geo. But there *are* Hufbands, Sir, who would rather have correƈted than amended your comparifon ; I, for inftance, fhould confider a man's complimenting my Wife as an impertinence.

Flut. Why, what harm can there be in compliments ? Sure they are not infeƈtious ; and, if they were, you, Sir George, of all people breathing, have reafon to be fatiffied about your Lady's attachment ; every body talks of it : that little Bird there, that fhe killed out of jealoufy, the moft extraordinary inftance of affeƈtion, that ever was given.

Lady Fran. I kill a Bird through jealoufy !—Heavens ! Mr. Flutter, how can you impute fuch a cruelty to me ?

Sir Geo. I could have forgiven you, if you had.

Flut. Oh, what a blundering Fool !—No, no—now I remember — 'twas your Bird, Lady Frances — that's it ;

your

your Bullfinch, which Sir George, in one of the refine-
ments of his passion, sent into the wide world to seek its
fortune.—He took it for a Knight in disguise.

Lady Fran. Is it possible! O, Sir George, could I
have imagin'd it was you who depriv'd me of a creature I
was so fond of?

Sir Geo. Mr. Flutter, you are one of those busy, idle,
meddling people, who, from mere vacuity of mind, are,
the most dangerous inmates in a family. You have neither
feelings nor opinions of your own; but, like a glass in a
tavern, bear about those of every Blockhead, who gives
you his;—and, because you *mean* no harm, think your-
selves excus'd, though broken friendships, discords,
and murders, are the consequences of your indiscretions.

Flut. (*taking out his Tablets*) Vacuity of Mind!—
What was the next? I'll write down this sermon; 'tis
the first I have heard since my Grandmother's funeral.

Miss Ogle. Come, Lady Frances, you see what a cruel
creature your loving Husband can be; so let us leave
him.

Sir Geo. Madam, Lady Frances shall not go.

Lady Fran. Shall not, Sir George?—This is the first
time such an expression—(*weeping*)

Sir Geo. My love! my life!

Lady Fran. Don't imagine I'll be treated like a Child!
denied what I wish, and then pacified with sweet words.

Miss Ogle (apart). The Bullfinch! that's an excellent subject; never let it down.

Lady Fran. I see plainly you would deprive me of
every pleasure, as well as of my sweet Bird—out of pure
love!—Barbarous Man!

Sir Geo. 'Tis well, Madam;—your resentment of that
circumstance proves to me, what I did not before sus-
pect, that you are deficient both in tenderness and un-
derstanding.—Tremble to think the hour approaches, in
which you would give worlds for such a proof of my
love. Go, Madam, give yourself to the Public; aban-

don

don your heart to diffipation, and fee if, in the fcenes
of gaiety and folly that await you, you can find a re-
compence for the loft affection of a doating Hufband.

[*Exit* Sir George.

Flut. Lord! what a fine thing it is to have the gift of
Speech! I fuppofe Sir George practifes at Coachmakers-
hall, or the Black-horfe in Bond-ftreet.

Lady Fran. He is really angry; I cannot go.

Mrs. Rack. Not go! Foolifh Creature! you are arrived at the moment, which fome time or other was fure to
happen; and every thing depends on the ufe you make of it.

Mifs Ogle. Come, Lady Frances! don't hefitate!—
the minutes are precious.

Lady Fran. I could find in my heart!—and yet I
won't give up neither.—If I fhould in this inftance, he'll
expect it for ever.

[*Exeunt Lady* Frances, *and Mrs.* Racket.

Mifs Ogle. Now you act like a Woman of Spirit.

[*Exeunt Mifs* Ogles, *and Mrs.* Racket.

Flut. A fair tug, by Jupiter—between Duty and Pleafure!—Pleafure beats, and off we go, *Iö triumphe!*

[*Exit* Flutter.

*Scene changes to an Auction Room.—Bufts, Pictures, &c. &c.
Enter* Silvertongue *with three Puffers.*

Sil. Very well,—very well.—This morning will be devoted to curiofity; my fale begins to-morrow at eleven.
But, Mrs. Fagg, if you do no better than you did in Lord
Fillagree's fale, I fhall difcharge you. — You want a
knack terribly: and this drefs—why, nobody can miftake
you for a Gentlewoman.

Fag. Very true, Mr. Silvertongue; but I can't drefs
like a Lady upon Half-a-crown a day, as the faying is—
If you want me to drefs like a Lady, you muft double my
pay.——Double or quits, Mr. Silvertongue.

Silv.——*Five Shillings* a day! what a demand! Why,
Woman, there are a thoufand Parfons in the town, who
don't

don't make Five Shilllings a day ; though they preach,
pray, chriften, marry, and bury, for the Good of the Com-
munity.—Five Shillings a day !—why, 'tis the pay of a
Lieutenant in a marching Regiment, who keeps a Servant, a Miftrefs, a Horfe ; fights, dreffes, ogles, makes
love, and dies upon Five Shillings a day.

Fag. Oh, as to that, all that's very right. A Soldier
fhould not be too fond of life ; and forcing him to do all
thefe things upon Five Shillings a day, is the readieft way
to make him tir'd on't.

Silv. Well, Mafk, have you been looking into the An-
tiquaries ?—have you got all the terms of art in a ftring
—aye ?

Mafk. Yes, I have : I know the Age of a Coin by the
tafte ; and can fix the Birth-day of a Medal, *Anno Mundi*
or *Anno Domini*, though the green ruft fhould have eaten up
every character. But you know, the brown fuit and
the wig I wear when I perfonate the Antiquary, are in
Limbo.

Silv. Thofe you have on, may do.

Mafk. Thefe!—Why, in thefe I am a young travell'd
Cognofcento : Mr. Glib bought them of Sir Tom Tot-
ter's Valet ; and I am going there directly. You know
his Picture-Sale comes on to-day ; and I have got my
head full of Parmegiano, Sal Rofa, Metzu, Tarback,
and Vandermeer. I talk of the relief of Woovermans,
the fpirit of Teniers, the colouring of the Venetian
School, and the correctnefs of the Roman. I diftinguifh
Claude by his Sleep, and Ruyfdael by his Water. The
rapidity of Tintoret's pencil ftrikes me at the firft glance ;
whilft the harmony of Vandyk, and the glow of Correggio,
point out their Mafters.

Enter Company.

1ſt Lady. Hey-day, Mr. Silvertongue! what, nobody
here !

Silv. Oh, my Lady, we fhall have company enough
in

in a trice ; if your carriage is feen at my door, no other will pafs it, I am fure.

1ft Lady. Familiar Monfter ! [*Afide*] That's a beautiful Diana, Mr. Silvertongue ; but in the name of Wonder, how came Actæon to be placed on the top of a Houfe ?

Silv. That's a David and Bathfheba, Ma'am.

Lady. Oh, I crave their pardon !—— I remember the Names, but know nothing of the Story.

More Company enters.

1ft Gent. Was not that Lady Frances Touchwood, coming up with Mrs. Racket ?

2d Gent. I think fo ;——yes, it is, faith.——Let us go nearer.

Enter Lady Frances, *Mrs.* Racket, *and Mifs* Ogle.

Silv. Yes, Sir, this is to be the firft Lot :—the Model of a City, in wax.

2d Gent. The Model of a City ! What City ?

Silv. That I have not been able to difcover ; but call it Rome, Pekin, or London, 'tis ftill a City : you'll find in it the fame jarring interefts, the fame paffions, the fame virtues, and the fame vices, whatever the name.

Gent. You may as well prefent us a Map of *Terra Incognita.*

Silv. Oh, pardon me, Sir ! a lively imagination would convert this waxen City into an endlefs and interefting amufement. For inftance—look into this little Houfe on the right-hand; there are four old Prudes in it, taking care of their Neighbours Reputations. This elegant Manfion on the left, decorated with Corinthian pillars — who needs be told that it belongs to a Court Lord, and is the habitation of Patriotifm, Philofophy, and Virtue ? Here's a City Hall—the rich fteams that iffue from the windows, nourifh a neighbouring Work-Houfe. Here's a Church— we'll pafs over that, the doors are fhut. The Parfonage-houfe comes next ;—we'll take a peep here, however.——

Look

Look at the Doctor! he's afleep on a volume of Toland;
whilft his Lady is putting on *rouge* for the Mafquerade.——
Oh! oh! this can be no Englifh City; our Parfons are
all orthodox, and their Wives the daughters of Modefty
and Meeknefs.

Lady Frances *and Mifs* Ogle *come forward, followed by*
Courtall.

Lady Fran. I wifh Sir George was here.——This man
follows me about, and ftares at me in fuch a way, that I
am quite uneafy.

Mifs Ogle. He has travell'd, and is heir to an immenfe
eftate; fo he's impertinent by Patent.

Court. You are very cruel, Ladies. Mifs Ogle—you
will not let me fpeak to you. As to this little fcornful
Beauty, fhe has frown'd me dead fifty times.

Lady Fran. Sir—I am a married Woman. *(Confus'd.)*

Court. A married Woman! a good hint. *(Afide.)*
'Twould be a fhame if fuch a charming Woman was not
married. But I fee you are a Daphne juft come from your
fheep, and your meadows; your crook, and your water-
falls. Pray now, who is the happy Damon, to whom you
have vow'd eternal truth and conftancy?

Mifs Ogle. 'Tis Lady Frances Touchwood, Mr. Courtall, to whom you are fpeaking.

Court. Lady Frances! By Heaven, that's Saville's old
flame. [*Afide*] I beg your Ladyfhip's pardon. I ought
to have believed that fuch beauty could belong only to
your Name——a Name I have long been enamour'd of;
becaufe I knew it to be that of the fineft Woman in the
world.

Mrs. Racket *comes forward.*

Lady Fran. [*Apart*] My dear Mrs. Racket, I am fo
frighten'd! Here's a Man making love to me, though he
knows I am married.

Mrs. Rack. Oh, the fooner for that, my dear; don't

F   mind

mind him. Was you at the *Caſſino* laſt night, Mr. Courtall ?

Court. I look'd in.——'Twas impoſſible to ſtay. No body there but Antiques. You'll be at Lady Brilliant's to-night, doubtleſs ?

Mrs. Rack. Yes, I go with Lady Frances.

Lady Fran. Bleſs me ! I did not know this Gentleman was acquainted with Mrs. Racket.—I behaved ſo rude to him ! [*To Miſs Ogle.*]

Mrs. Rack. Come, Ma'am ; [*looking at her Watch*] 'tis paſt one. I proteſt, if we don't fly to Kenſington, we ſha'n't find a ſoul there.

Lady Fran. Won't this Gentleman go with us ?

Court. [*Looking ſurpris'd.*] To be ſure, you make me happy, Ma'am, beyond deſcription.

Mrs. Rack. Oh, never mind him—he'll follow.

[*Exeunt Lady* Frances, *Mrs.* Racket, *and Miſs* Ogle.

Court. Lady *Touchwood !* with a vengeance ! But, 'tis always ſo ;—your reſerved Ladies are like Ice, 'egad !— no ſooner begin to ſoften, than they melt.

[*Following.*

END OF THE SECOND ACT.

ACT III.

SCENE I. *Mr.* Hardy's.

Enter Letitia *and Mrs.* Racket.

Mrs. Racket.

COME, prepare, prepare ; your Lover is coming.

Let. My Lover !—Confeſs now that my abſence at dinner was a ſevere mortificat to him.

Mrs.

Mrs. Rack. I can't abfolutely fwear it fpoilt his appetite; he eat as if he was hungry, and drank his wine as though he liked it.

Letit. What was the apology?

Mrs. Rack. That you were ill;—but I gave him a hint, that your extreme bafhfulnefs could not fupport his eye.

Letit. If I comprehend him, aukwardnefs and bafhfulnefs are the laft faults he can pardon in a woman; fo expect to fee me transform'd into the verieft maukin.

Mrs. Rack. You perfevere then?

Letit. Certainly. I know the defign is a rafh one, and the event important;—it either makes Doricourt mine by all the tendereft ties of paffion, or deprives me of him for ever; and never to be his wife will afflict me lefs, than to be his wife and not be belov'd.

Mrs. Rack. So you wo'n't truft to the good old maxim—" Marry firft, and love will follow?"

Letit. As readily as I would venture my laft guinea, that good fortune might follow. The woman that has not touch'd the heart of a man before he leads her to the altar, has fcarcely a chance to charm it when, poffeffion and fecurity turn their powerful arms againft her.—But here he comes.—I'll difappear for a moment.—Don't fpare me.

[*Exit* Letitia.

Enter Doricourt *(not feeing Mrs.* Racket.)

Doric. So! [*Looking at a Picture.*] this is my miftrefs, I prefume.—*Ma foi!* the painter has hit her off.—The downcaft eye—the blufhing cheek—timid—apprehenfive —bafhful.—A tear and a prayer-book would have made her *La Bella Magdalena.*—

Give *me* a woman in whofe touching mien
A mind, a foul, a polifh'd art is feen;
Whofe motion fpeaks, whofe peignant air can move.
Such are the darts to wound with endlefs love.

Mrs.

Mrs. Rack. Is that an impromptu? [*Touching him on the shoulder with her fan.*]

Doric. (*starting.*) Madam!—[*Aside.*] Finely caught! —Not absolutely—it struck me during the dessert, as a motto for your picture.

Mrs. Rack. Gallantly turn'd! I perceive, however, Miss Hardy's charms have made no violent impression on you.—And who can wonder?—the poor girl's defects are so obvious.

Doric. Defects!

Mrs. Rack. Merely those of education.—Her father's indulgence ruin'd her.—*Mauvaise honte*—conceit and ig-norance—all unite in the Lady you are to marry.

Doric. Marry!—I marry such a woman!—Your pic-ture, I hope, is overcharged.—I marry *mauvaise honte*, pertness and ignorance!

Mrs. Rack. Thank your stars, that ugliness and ill temper are not added to the list.—You must think her handsome?

Doric. Half her personal beauty would content me; but could the Medicean Venus be animated for me, and endowed with a vulgar soul, *I* should become the statue, and my heart transform'd to marble.

Mrs. Rack. Bless us!—We are in a hopeful **way** then!

Doric. (*Aside.*) There must be some envy in this!— I see she is a coquette. Ha, ha, ha! And you imagine I am persuaded of the truth of your character? ha, ha, ha! Miss Hardy, I have been assur'd, Madam, is elegant and accomplished:——but one **must** allow for a Lady's painting.

Mrs. Rack. (*Aside.*) I'll be even with him for that. Ha! ha! ha! and so you have found me out!—Well, I protest I meant no harm; 'twas only to increase the *éclat* of her appearance, that I threw a veil over her charms.——Here comes the Lady;—her elegance and accomplishments will announce themselves. *Enter*

Enter Letitia, *running.*

Let. La! Coufin, do you know that our John——oh, dear heart!—I didn't fee you, Sir. (*Hanging down her head, and dropping behind Mrs.* Racket.)

Mrs. Rack. Fye, Letitia! Mr. Doricourt thinks you a woman of elegant manners. Stand forward, and confirm his opinion.

Let. No, no; keep before me.——He's my Sweetheart; and 'tis impudent to look one's Sweetheart in the face, you know.

Mrs. Rack. You'll allow in future for a Lady's painting, Sir. Ha! ha! ha!

Doric. I am aftonifh'd!

Let. Well, hang it, I'll take heart.—Why, he is but a Man, you know, Coufin;—and I'll let him fee I was'nt born in a Wood to be fcar'd by an Owl. [*Half apart; advances, and looks at him through her fingers.*] He! he! he! [*Goes up to him, and makes a very ftiff formal curtefy.*]— [*He bows*]—You have been a great Traveller, Sir, I hear?

Dor. Yes, Madam.

Let. Then I wifh you'd tell us about the fine fights you faw when you went over-fea.—I have read in a book, that there are fome countries where the Men and Women are all Horfes.—Did you fee any of them?

Mrs. Rack. Mr. Doricourt is not prepared, my dear, for thefe enquiries; he is reflecting on the importance of the queftion, and will anfwer you——when he can.

Let. When he can! Why, he's as flow in fpeech, as Aunt Margery, when fhe's reading Thomas Aquinas;— and ftands gaping like mum-chance.

Mrs. Rack. Have a little difcretion.

Let. Hold your tongue!—Sure I may fay what I pleafe before I am married, if I can't afterwards.—D'ye think a body does not know how to talk to a Sweetheart. He is not the firft I have had.

Dor. Indeed!

Let.

Let. Oh, Lud ! He fpeaks!—Why, if you muft know—there was the Curate at home :—when Papa was a-hunting, he ufed to come a fuitoring, and make fpeeches to me out of books.—No body knows what a *mort* of fine things he ufed to fay to me ;—and call me Venis, and Jubah, and Dinah !

Dor. And pray, fair Lady, how did you anfwer him ?

Let. Why, I ufed to fay, Look you, Mr. Curate, don't think to come over me with your flim-flams ; for a better Man than ever trod in your fhoes, is coming over-fea to marry me ;—but, ifags ! I begin to think I was out.—Parfon Dobbins was the fprightfuller man of the two.

Dor. Surely this cannot be Mifs Hardy !

Let. Laws ! why, don't you know me ! You faw me to-day—but I was daunted before my Father, and the Lawyer, and all them, and did not care to fpeak out :—fo, may be, you thought I couldn't ;—but I can talk as faft as any body, when I know folks a little :—and now I have fhewn my parts, I hope you'll like me better.

Enter Hardy.

Har. I forefee this won't do !—Mr. Doricourt, may be you take my Daughter for a Fool ; but your are miftaken : fhe's a fenfible Girl as any in England.

Dor. I am convinced fhe has a very uncommon underftanding, Sir. [*Afide*] I did not think he had been fuch an Afs.

Let. My Father will undo the whole.—Laws ! Papa, how can you think he can take me for a fool ! when every body knows I beat the Potecary at Conundrums laft Chriftmas-time ? and did'nt I make a ftring of names, all in riddles, for the Lady's Diary ?—There was a little River, and a great Houfe ; that was Newcaftle.—There was what a Lamb fays, and three Letters ; that was *Ba,* and *k-e-r,* ker, Baker.—There was—

Hardy. Don't ftand ba-a-ing there. You'll make me mad in a moment !—I tell you, Sir, that for all that, fhe's dev'lifh fenfible.

Doric.

Doric. Sir, I give all poffible credit to your affertions.

Letit. Laws! Papa, do come along. If you ftand watching, how can my Sweetheart break his mind, and tell me how he admires me?

Doric. That would be difficult, indeed, Madam.

Hardy. I tell you, Letty, I'll have no more of this.—— I fee well enough——

Letit. Laws! don't fnub me before my Hufband—that is is to be.—You'll teach him to fnub me too,—and I believe, by his looks, he'd like to begin now.—So, let us go, Coufin; you may tell the Gentleman what a genus I have—how I can cut Watch-papers, and work Cat-gut; make Quadrille-bafkets with Pins, and take Profiles in Shade; ay, as well as the Lady at N°. 62, South Moulton-ftreet, Grofvenor-fquare.   [*Ex.* Hardy *and* Letitia.

Mrs. Rack. What think you of my painting, now?

Doric. Oh, mere water-colours, Madam! The Lady has caricatured your picture.

Mrs. Rack. And how does fhe like you on the whole?

Doric. Like a good Defign, fpoilt by the incapacity of the Artift. Her faults are evidently the refult of her Father's weak indulgence. I obferve an expreffion in her eye, that feemed to fatyrife the folly of her lips.

Mrs. Rack. But at her age, when Education is fixed, and Manner becomes Nature—hopes of improvement—

Doric. Would be as rational, as hopes of Gold from a Jugler's Crucible.—Doricourt's Wife muft be incapable of improvement; but it muft be becaufe fhe's got beyond it.

Mrs. Rack. I am pleafed your misfortune fits no heavier.

Doric. Your pardon, Madam; fo mercurial was the hour in which I was born, that misfortunes always go plump to the bottom of my heart, like a pebble in water, and leave the furface unruffled.—I fhall certainly fet off for Bath, or the other world, to-night;—but whether I fhall ufe a chaife with four fwift courfers, or go off in a

tangent—

tangent—from the aperture of a piftol, deferves confider-
ation ; fo I make my *adieus.* (*Going.*)

Mrs. Rack. Oh, but I intreat you, poftpone your jour-
ney 'till to-morrow ; determine on which you will—you
muft be this night at the Mafquerade.

Doric. Mafquerade !

Mrs. Rack. Why not ?—If you refolve to vifit the
other world, you may as well take one night's pleafure
firft in this, you know.

Doric. Faith, that's very true ; Ladies are the beft
Philofophers, after all. Expect me at the Mafquerade.

[Exit Doricourt.

Mrs. Rack. He's a charming Fellow !—I think Letitia fha'n't have him. (*Going.*)

Enter Hardy.

Hardy. What's he gone ?

Mrs. Rack. Yes ; and I am glad he is. You would
have ruined us !—Now, I beg, Mr. Hardy, you won't in-
terfere in this bufinefs ; it is a little out of your way.

[Exit Mrs. Racket.

Hardy. Hang me, if I don't though. I forefee very
clearly what will be the end of it, if I leave ye to your-
felves ; fo, I'll e'en follow him to the Mafquerade, and
tell him all about it : Let me fee.—What fhall my drefs
be ? A Great Mogul ? No.—A Grenadier ? No ;—no,
that, I forefee, would make a laugh. Hang me, if I don't
fend to my favourite little Quick, and borrow his
Jew Ifaac's drefs :—I know the Dog likes a glafs of good
wine ; fo I'll give him a bottle of my Forty-eight, and he
fhall teach me. Aye, that's it—I'll be Cunning Little
Ifaac ! If they complain of my want of wit, I'll tell
'em the curfed Duenna wears the breeches, and has fpoilt
my parts.   [*Exit* Hardy.

Enter Courtall, Saville, *and three others, from an Apartment in the back Scene.* (*The last three tipsey.*)

Court. You shan't go yet :——Another catch, and another bottle !

First Gent. May I be a bottle, and an empty bottle, if you catch me at that !—Why, I am going to the Masquerade. Jack ——, you know who I mean, is to meet me, and we are to have a leap at the new lustres.

Second Gent. And I am going too—a Harlequin—— (*hiccups*) Am not I in a pretty pickle to make Harlequinades ?——And Tony, here—he is going in the disguise—in the disguise—of a Gentleman !

First Gent. We are all very disguised ; so bid them draw up—D'ye hear !

[*Exeunt the three Gentlemen.*

Sav. Thy skull, Courtall, is a Lady's thimble :—no, an egg-shell.

Court. Nay, then you are gone too ; you never aspire to similes, but in your cups.

Sav. No, no ; I am steady enough—but the fumes of the wine pass directly through thy egg-shell, and leave thy brain as cool as——Hey ! I am quite sober ; my similes fail me.

Court. Then we'll sit down here, and have one sober bottle.—Bring a table and glasses.

Sav. I'll not swallow another drop ; no, though the juice should be the true Falernian.

Court. By the bright eyes of her you love, you shall drink her health.

Sav. Ah ! (*sitting down*) Her I loved is gone (*sighing.*)— She's married !

Court. Then bless your stars you are not her Husband !

G I would

I would be Hufband to no Woman in Europe, who was not dev'lifh rich, and dev'lifh ugly.

Sav. Wherefore ugly ?

Court. Becaufe fhe could not have the confcience to exact thofe attentions that a Pretty Wife expects; or, if fhe fhould, her refentments would be perfectly eafy to me, nobody would undertake to revenge her caufe.

Sav. Thou art a moft licentious fellow !

Court. I fhould hate my own wife, that's certain; but I have a warm heart for thofe of other people; and fo here's to the pretticft Wife in England—Lady Frances Touchwood.

Sav. Lady Frances Touchwood ! I rife to drink her. *(drinks)* How the devil came Lady Frances in your head ? I never knew you give a Woman of Chaftity before.

Court. That's odd, for you have heard me give half the Women of Fafhion in England.—But, pray now, what do you take a Woman of Chaftity to be ? *(fneeringly.)*

Sav. Such a woman as Lady Frances Touchwood, Sir.

Court. Oh, you are grave, Sir ; I remember you was an Adorer of her's—Why did'nt you marry her ?

Sav. I had not the arrogance to look fo high—Had my fortune been worthy of her, fhe fhould not have been ignorant of my admiration.

Court. Precious fellow ! What, I fuppofe you would not dare tell her now that you admire her ?

Sav. No, nor you.

Court. By the Lord, I have told her fo.

Sav. Have ! Impoffible !

Court. Ha ! ha ! ha !—Is it fo ?

Sav. How did fhe receive the declaration?

Court. Why, in the old way; blufhed, and frowned, and faid fhe was married.

Sav. What amazing things thou art capable of ! I
could

could more eafily have taken the Pope by the beard, than prophaned her ears with fuch a declaration.

Court. I fhall meet her at Lady Brilliant's to-night, where I fhall repeat it; and I'll lay my life, under a mafk, fhe'll hear it all without blufh, or frown.

Sav. (*rifing*) 'Tis falfe, Sir!—She won't.

Court. She will! (*rifing*) Nay, I'd venture to lay a round fum, that I prevail on her to go out with me —— only to tafte the frefh air, I mean.

Sav. Prepofterous vanity! From this moment I fufpect that half the victories you have boafted, are falfe and flanderous, as your pretended influence with Lady Frances.

Court. Pretended!—How fhould fuch a Fellow as you, now, who never foared beyond a cherry-checked Daughter of a Ploughman in Norfolk, judge of the influence of a Man of my Figure and Habits? I could fhew thee a lift, in which there are names to fhake thy faith in the whole fex!—and, to that lift I have no doubt of adding the name of Lady ————

Sav. Hold, Sir! My ears cannot bear the profanation; —you cannot—dare not approach her!—For your foul you dare not mention Love to her! Her look would freeze the word, whilft it hovered on thy licentious lips!

Court. Whu! whu! Well, we fhall fee—this evening, by Jupiter, the trial fhall be made—if I fail—I fail.

Sav. I think thou dareft not!—But my life, my honour on her purity. [*Exit Saville.*

Court. Hot-headed fool! But fince he has brought it to this point, by Gad I'll try what can be done with her Ladyfhip (*mufing*)—(*rings*) She's froft-work, and the prejudices of education yet ftrong: *ergo*, paffionate profeffions will only inflame her pride, and put her on her guard.—For other arts then!

Entsr

Enter Dick.

Dick, do you know any of the fervants at Sir George
Touchwood's ?

Dick. Yes, Sir; I knows the Groom, and one of the
Houfe-maids : for the matter-o'-that, fhe's my own
Coufin; and it was my Mother that holp'd her to the
place.

Court. Do you know Lady Frances's Maid ?

Dick. I can't fay as how I know fhe.

Court. Do you know Sir George's Valet ?

Dick. No, Sir; but Sally is very thick with Mr. Gibfon, Sir George's Gentleman.

Court. Then go there directly, and employ Sally to
difcover whether her Mafter goes to Lady Brilliant's this
evening ; and, if he does, the name of the fhop that fold
his Habit.

Dick. Yes, Sir.

Court. Be exact in your intelligence, and come to me
at Boodle's: [*Exit* Dick.] If I cannot otherwife fucceed, I'll beguile her as Jove did Alcmena, in the fhape
of her Hufband. The poffeffion of fo fine a Woman —
the triumph over Saville, are each a fufficient motive ;
and united, they fhall be refiftlefs.

[*Exit* Courtall.

S C E N E III. ——— *The Street.*

Enter Saville.

Sav. The air has recover'd me ! What have I been
doing ! Perhaps my petulance may be the caufe of *her*
ruin, whofe honour I afferted :—his vanity is piqued ;—
and where Women are concerned, Courtall can be a
villain.

Enter Dick. *Bows, and paffes haftily.*

Ha ! that's his Servant !——Dick !

Dick. [*returning*] Sir.

Sav. Where are you going, Dick ?

Dick.

Dick. Going! I am going, Sir, where my Mafter
fent me.

Sav. Well anfwer'd;—but I have a particular reafon
for my enquiry, and you muft tell me.

Dick. Why then, Sir, I am going to call upon a Coufin of mine, that lives at Sir George Touchwood's.

Sav. Very well.—There, [*gives him money*] you muft
make your Coufin drink my health.—What are you going
about?

Dick. Why, Sir, I believe 'tis no harm, or elfeways I
am fure I would not blab.—I am only going to ax if Sir
George goes to the Mafquerade to-night, and what Drefs
he wears.

Sav. Enough! Now, Dick, if you will call at my
lodgings in your way back, and acquaint me with your
Coufin's intelligence, I'll double the trifle I have given
you.

Dick. Blefs your honour, I'll call——never fear.

[*Exit* Dick.

Sav. Surely the occafion may juftify the means:—'tis
doubly my duty to be Lady Frances's Protector. Courtall, I fee, is planning an artful fcheme; but Saville fhall
out-plot him. [*Exit* Saville.

SCENE IV.——*Sir* George Touchwood's.

Enter Sir George *and* Villers.

Vill. For fhame, Sir George! you have left Lady Frances in tears.—How can you afflict her?

Sir Geo. 'Tis I that am afflicted;—my dream of happinefs is over.—Lady Frances and I are difunited.

Vill. The Devil! Why, you have been in town but
ten days: fhe can have made no acquaintance for a Com-
mons affair yet.

Sir Geo. Pho! 'tis our minds that are difunited: fhe
no longer places her whole delight in me; fhe has yielded herfelf up to the world!

Vill.

Vill. Yielded herfelf up to the World ! Why did you not bring her to town in a Cage ? Then fhe might have taken a peep at the World !—But, after all, what has the World done ? A twelvemonth fince you was the gayeft fellow in it :—If any body afk'd who dreffes beft ?—Sir George Touchwood.—Who is the moft gallant Man ? Sir George Touchwood.—Who is the moft wedded to Amufement and Diffipation ? Sir George Touchwood.— And now Sir George is metamorphofed into a four Cenfor ; and talks of Fafhionable Life with as much bitternefs, as the old crabbed Fellow in Rome.

Sir Geo. The moment I became poffeffed of fuch a jewel as Lady Frances, every thing wore a different complexion: that Society in which I liv'd with fo much *éclat*, became the object of my terror ; and I think of the manners of Polite Life, as I do of the atmofphere of a Pefthoufe.—My Wife is already infected ; fhe was fet upon this morning by Maids, Widows, and Bachelors, who carried her off in triumph, in fpite of my difpleafure.

Vill. Aye, to be fure ; there would have been no triumph in the cafe, if you had not oppos'd it :—but I have heard the whole ftory from Mrs. Rackett ; and I affure you, Lady Frances didn't enjoy the morning at all ;—fhe wifh'd for you fifty times.

Sir Geo. Indeed ! Are you fure of that ?

Vill. Perfectly fure.

Sir Geo. I wifh I had known it :——my uneafinefs at dinner was occafioned by very different ideas.

Vill. Here then fhe comes, to receive your apology ; but if fhe is true Woman, her difpleafure will rife in proportion to your contrition ; — and till you grow carelefs about her pardon, fhe won't grant it : —— however, I'll leave you.——Matrimonial Duets are feldom fet in the ftyle I like.   [*Exit* Villers.

Enter Lady Frances.

Sir Geo. The fweet forrow that glitters in thefe eyes, I
cannot

cannot bear *(embracing her)*. Look chearfully, you Rogue.

Lady Fran. I cannot look otherwife, if you are pleas'd with me.

Sir Geo. Well, Fanny, to-day you made your *entrée* in the Fafhionable World; tell me honeftly the impreffions you receiv'd.

Lady Fran. Indeed, Sir George, I was fo hurried from place to place, that I had not time to find out what my impreffions were.

Sir Geo. That's the very fpirit of the life you have chofen.

Lady Fran. Every body about me feem'd happy—but every body feem'd in a hurry to be happy fomewhere elfe.

Sir Geo. And you like this?

Lady Fran. One muft like what the reft of the World likes.

Sir Geo. Pernicious maxim!

Lady Fran. But, my dear Sir George, you have not promis'd to go with me to the Mafquerade.

Sir Geo. 'Twould be a fhocking indecorum to be feen together, you know.

Lady Fran. Oh, no; I afk'd Mrs. Racket, and fhe told me we might be feen together at the Mafquerade—without being laugh'd at.

Sir Geo. Really?

Lady Fran. Indeed, to tell you the truth, I could wifh it was the fafhion for married people to be infeparable; for I have more heart-felt fatisfaction in fifteen minutes with you at my fide, than fifteen days of amufement could give me without you.

Sir Geo. My fweet Creature! How that confeffion charms me!—Let us begin the Fafhion.

Lady Fran. O, impoffible! We fhould not gain a fingle profelyte; and you can't conceive what fpiteful things would be faid of us.—At Kenfington to-day a Lady met us, whom we faw at Court, when we were prefented; fhe
lifted

lifted up her hands in amazement !——Blefs me ! faid fhe
to her companion, here's Lady Francis without Sir Hurlo
Thrumbo !—My dear Mrs. Racket, confider what an important charge you have ! for Heaven's fake take her
home again, or fome Enchanter on a flying Dragon will
defcend and carry her off. — Oh, faid another, I dare
fay Lady Frances has a clue at her heel, like the peerlefs
Rofamond :—her tender fwain would never have trufted
her fo far without fuch a precaution.

Sir Geo. Heav'n and Earth !——How fhall Innocence
preferve its luftre amidft manners fo corrupt !— My dear
Fanny, I feel a fentiment for thee at this moment, tenderer
than Love — more animated than Paffion.——I could
weep over that purity, expos'd to the fullying breath
of Fafhion, and the *Ton*, in whofe latitudinary vortex
Chaftity herfelf can fcarcely move unfpotted.

Enter Gibfon.

Gib. Your Honour talk'd, I thought, fomething about
going to the Mafquerade ?

Sir Geo. Well.

Gib. Isn't it ?—hasn't your Honour ?—I thought your
Honour had forgot to order a Drefs.

Lady Fran. Well confider'd, Gibfon.—Come, will you
be Jew, Turk, or Heretic ; a Chinefe Emperor, or a
Ballad-Singer ; a Rake, or a Watchman ?

Sir Geo. Oh, neither, my Love ; I can't take the trouble
to fupport a character.

Lady Fran. You'll wear a Domino then :—I faw a
pink Domino trimm'd with blue at the fhop where I
bought my Habit.—Would you like it ?

Sir Geo. Any thing, any thing.

Lady Fran. Then go about it directly, Gibfon.——A
pink Domino trimm'd with blue, and a Hat of the fame—
Come, you have not feen my Drefs yet—it is moft beautiful; I long to have it on.

[Exeunt Sir George and Lady Frances.
Gib.

Gib. A pink Domino trimm'd with blue, and a Hat of the fame——What the devil can it fignify to Sally now what his Drefs is to be ?—Surely the Slut has not made an affignation to meet her Mafter !

[*Exit* Gibfon.

END of the THIRD ACT.

ACT IV.

SCENE——*A Mafquerade.*

A Party dancing Cotillons in front—a variety of Characters pafs and repafs.

Enter Folly *en a Hobby-Horfe, with Cap and Bells.*

Mafk.

HEY ! Tom Fool ! what bufinefs have you here ?
   Foll. What, Sir ! Affront a Prince in his own Dominions !
[*Struts off.*

Mountebank. Who'll buy my Noftrums ? Who'll buy my Noftrums ?

Mafk. What are they ? *(They all come round him.)*

Mount. Different forts, and for different cuftomers. Here's a Liquor for Ladies—it expels the rage of Gaming and Gallantry. Here's a Pill for Members of Parliament —good to fettle Confciences. Here's an Eye-Water for Jealous Hufbands—it thickens the Vifual Membrane, through which they fee too clearly. Here's a Decoction for the Clergy—it never fits eafy, if the patient has more than One Living. Here's a Draught for Lawyers—a great promoter of Modefty. Here's a Powder for Projectors—'twill rectify the fumes of an Empty Stomach, and diffipate their airy caftles.

H   *Mafk.*

Mask. Have you a Noftrum that can give patience to Young Heirs, whofe Uncles and Fathers are ftout and healthy?

Mount. Yes; and I have an Infufion for Creditors— it gives refignation and humility, when Fine Gentlemen break their promifes, or plead their privilege.

Mask. Come along:—I'll find you cuftomers for your whole cargo.

Enter Hardy, *in the Drefs of* Ifaac Mendoza.

Hardy. Why, isn't it a fhame to fee fo many ftout, well-built Young Fellows, mafquerading, and cutting *Couranta's* here at home—inftead of making the French cut capers to the tune of your Cannon—or fweating the Spaniards with an Englifh *Fandango?*—I forefee the end of all this.

Mask. Why, thou little tefty Ifraelite! back to Duke's Place; and preach your tribe into a fubfcription for the good of the land on whofe milk and honey ye fatten. — Where are your Jofhuas and your Gideons, aye? What! all dwindled into Stockbrokers, Pedlars, and Rag-Men?

Har. No, not all. Some of us turn Chriftians, and by degrees grow into all the privileges of Englifhmen! In the fecond generation we are Patriots, Rebels, Courtiers, and Hufbands. [*Puts his fingers to his forehead.*]

Two other Mafks advance.

3d Mafk. What, my little Ifaac!——How the Devil came you here? Where's your old Margaret?

Har. Oh, I have got rid of her.

3d Mafk. How?

Har. Why, I perfuaded a young Irifhman that fhe was a blooming plump Beauty of eighteen; fo they made an Elopement, ha! ha! ha! and fhe is now the Toaft of Tipperary. Ha! there's Coufin Racket and her Party; they fha'n't know me.   [*Puts on his Mafk.*

Enter

Enter Mrs. Racket, *Lady* Frances, *Sir* George, *and* Flutter.

Mrs. Rack. Look at this dumpling Jew; he muſt be a Levite by his figure. . You have ſurely practiſed the fleſh-hook a long time, friend, to have raiſed that goodly preſence.

Har. About as long, my briſk Widow, as you have been angling for a ſecond Huſband; but my hook has been better baited than your's.—You have only caught Gudgeons, I ſee.   [*Pointing to* Flutter.

Flut. Oh! this is one of the Geniuſes they hire to en-tertain the Company with their *accidental* ſallies.——Let me look at your Common-Place Book, friend.—I want a few good things.

Har. I'd oblige you, with all my heart; but you'll ſpoil them in repeating—or, if you ſhou'd not, they'll gain you no reputation—for no body will believe they are your own.

Sir Geo. He knows ye, Flutter;—the little Gentleman fancies himſelf a Wit, I ſee.

Har. There's no depending on what *you* ſee—the eyes of the jealous are not to be truſted.—Look to your Lady.

Flut. He knows ye, Sir George.

Sir Geo. What! am I the Town-talk?   [*Aſide*]

Har. I can neither ſee Doricourt nor Letty.—I muſt find them out.   [*Exit* Hardy.

Mrs. Rack. Well, Lady Frances, is not all this charm-ing? Could you have conceived ſuch a brilliant aſſem-blage of objects?

Lady Fran. Delightful! The days of enchantment are reſtor'd; the columns glow with Sapphires and Rubies. Emperors and Fairies, Beauties and Dwarfs, meet me at every ſtep.

Sir Geo. How lively are firſt impreſſions on ſenſible minds! In four hours, vapidity and languor will take place of that exquiſite ſenſe of joy, which flutters your little heart.

Mrs.

Mrs. Rack. What an inhuman creature! Fate has not allow'd us these sensations above ten times in our lives; and would you have us shorten them by antici-pation?

Flut. O Lord! your Wife Men are the greatest Fools upon earth:—they reason about their enjoyments, and analyse their pleasures, whilst the essence escapes. Look, Lady Frances: D'ye see that Figure strutting in the dress of an Emperor? His Father retails Oranges in Botolph Lane. That Gypsey is a Maid of Honour, and that Rag-man a Physician.

Lady Fran. Why, you know every body.

Flut. Oh, every creature.—A Mask is nothing at all to me.—I can give you the history of half the people here. In the next apartment there's a whole family, who, to my knowledge, have lived on Water-Cresses this month, to make a figure here to-night;—but, to make up for that, they'll cram their pockets with cold Ducks and Chickens, for a Carnival to-morrow.

Lady Fran. Oh, I should like to see this provident Family.

Flut. Honour me with your arm.

[*Exeunt* Flutter *and Lady* Frances.

Mrs. Rack. Come, Sir George, you shall be *my* Beau. —We'll make the *tour* of the rooms, and meet them. Oh! your pardon, you must follow Lady Frances; or the wit and fine parts of Mr. Flutter may drive you out of her head. Ha! ha! ha!

[*Exit Mrs.* Rackett.

Sir Geo. I was going to follow her, and now I dare not. How can I be such a fool as to be govern'd by the *fear* of that ridicule which I despise!   [*Exit Sir* George.

Enter Doricourt, *meeting a Mask.*

Doric. Ha! my Lord!—I thought you had been enga-ged at Westminster on this important night.

Mask.

Mask. So I am—I flipt out as foon as Lord Trope got upon his legs; I can *badinage* here an hour or two, and be back again before he is down.——There's a fine Figure! I'll addrefs her.

Enter Letitia.

Charity, fair Lady! Charity for a poor Pilgrim.

Letit. Charity! If you mean my prayers, Heaven grant thee Wit, Pilgrim.

Mask. That blefling would do from a Devotee: from you I afk other charities;—fuch charities as Beauty fhould beftow—foft Looks—fweet Words—and kind Wifhes.

Letit. Alas! I am bankrupt of thefe, and forced to turn Beggar myfelf.——There he is!—how fhall I catch his attention?

Mask. Will you grant me no favour?

Letit. Yes, one—I'll make you my Partner—not for life, but through the foft mazes of a minuet.—Dare you dance?

Doric. Some fpirit in that.

Mask. I dare do any thing you command.

Doric. Do you know her, my Lord?

Mask. No: Such a woman as that, would formerly have been known in any difguife; but Beauty is now common—Venus feems to have given her *Ceftus* to the whole fex.

A Minuet.

Doric. (*during the Minuet*) She dances divinely.—(*When ended*) Somebody muft know her! Let us enquire who fhe is.   [*Exit.*

Enter Saville *and* Kitty Willis, *habited like Lady* Frances.

Sav. I have feen Courtall in Sir George's habit, though he endeavoured to keep himfelf conceal'd. Go, and feat yourfelf in the tea-room, and on no account difcover your face:—remember too, Kitty, that the Woman you are to perfonate is a Woman of Virtue.

Kitty. I am afraid I fhall find that a difficult character: indeed I believe it is feldom kept up through a whole Mafquerade.

Sav. Of that *you* can be no judge——Follow my directions, and you fhall be rewarded.   [*Exit* Kitty.

Enter Doricourt.

Dor. Ha! Saville! Did you fee a Lady dance juft now?

Sav. No.

Dor. Very odd.   No body knows her.

Sav. Where is Mifs Hardy?

Dor. Cutting Watch-papers, and making Conundrums, I fuppofe.

Sav. What do you mean?

Dor. Faith, I hardly know.   She's not here, however, Mrs. Racket tells me.—I afk'd no further.

Sav. Your indifference feems increas'd.

Dor. Quite the reverfe; 'tis advanced thirty-two degrees towards hatred.

Sav. You are jefting?

Dor. Then it muft be with a very ill grace, my dear Saville; for I never felt fo ferioufly: Do you know the creature's almoft an Ideot?

Sav. What!

Dor. An Ideot. What the devil fhall I do with her? Egad! I think I'll feign myfelf mad—and then Hardy will propofe to cancel the engagements.

Sav. An excellent expedient.   I muft leave you; you are myfterious, and I can't ftay to unravel ye. — I came here to watch over Innocence and Beauty.

Dor. The Guardian of Innocence and Beauty at three and twenty! Is there not a cloven foot under that black gown, Saville?

Sav. No, faith.   Courtall is here on a moft deteftable defign.—I found means to get a knowledge of the Lady's drefs, and have brought a girl to perfonate her, whofe
repu-

reputation cannot be hurt.—You ſhall know the reſult to-morrow. Adieu.　　　　　　　　　[*Exit* Saville.

Dor. (*muſing*) Yes, I think that will do.—I'll feign myſelf mad, fee the Doctor to pronounce me incurable, and when the parchments are deſtroyed————

[*As he ſtands in a muſing poſture,* Letitia *enters, and ſings.*]

S O N G.

Wake! thou Son of Dullneſs, wake!
　　From thy drowſy ſenſes ſhake
All the ſpells that Care employs,
　　Cheating Mortals of their joys.

II.

Light-wing'd Spirits, hither haſte!
　　Who prepare for mortal taſte
All the gifts that Pleaſure ſends,
　　Every bliſs that youth attends.

III.

Touch his feelings, rouze his ſoul,
　　Whilſt the ſparkling moments roll;
Bid them wake to new delight,
　　Crown the magic of the night.

Dor. By Heaven, the ſame ſweet creature!

Let. You have choſen an odd ſituation for ſtudy. Faſhion and Taſte preſide in this ſpot:—they throw their ſpells around you:—ten thouſand delights ſpring up at their command;—and you, a Stoic—a being without ſenſes, are wrapt in reflection.

Dor. And you, the moſt charming being in the world, awake me to admiration. Did you come from the Stars?

Let. Yes, and I ſhall reaſcend in a moment.

Dor. Pray ſhew me your face before you go.

Let. Beware of imprudent curioſity; it loſt Paradiſe.

Dor. Eve's curioſity was rais'd by the Devil;—'tis an Angel tempts mine.—So your alluſion is not in point.

　　　　　　　　　　　　　　　　　Let.

Let. But *why* would you fee my face ?

Dor. To fall in love with it.

Let. And what then ?

Dor. Why, then—Aye, curfe it! there's the rub. [*Afide.*]

Let. Your Miftrefs will be angry ;—but, perhaps, you have no Miftrefs ?

Dor. Yes, yes; and a fweet one it is !

Let. What ! is fhe old ?

Dor. No.

Let. Ugly ?

Dor. No.

Let. What then ?

Dor. Pho ! don't talk about *her*; but fhew me your face.

Let. My vanity forbids it ;—'twould frighten you.

Dor. Impoffible ! Your Shape is graceful, your Air bewitching, your Bofom tranfparent, and your Chin would tempt me to kifs it, if I did not fee a pouting red Lip above it, that demands————

Let. You grow too free.

Dor. Shew me your face then—only half a glance.

Let. Not for worlds.

Dor. What ! you will have a little gentle force? [*Attempts to feize her Mafk.*

Let. I am gone for ever ! [*Exit.*

Dor. 'Tis falfe ;—I'll follow to the end. [*Exit.*

Flutter, *Lady* Frances, *and* Saville *advance.*

Lady Fran. How can you be thus interefted for a ftranger ?

Sav. Goodnefs will ever intereft ; its home is Heaven : on earth 'tis but a Wanderer. Imprudent Lady ! why have you left the fide of your Protector ? Where is your Hufband ?

Flut. Why, what's that to him ?

Lady Fran. Surely it can't be merely his habit ;—— there's fomething in him that awes me.

Flut.

Flut. Pho ! 'tis only his grey beard.—I know him ; he keeps a Lottery-office on Cornhill.

Sav. My province, as an Enchanter, lays open every secret to me.   Lady ! there are dangers abroad—Beware !
                                                    [*Exit.*

Lady Fran. 'Tis very odd ; his manner has made me tremble.   Let us seek Sir George.

Flut. He is coming towards us.

Courtall *comes forward, habited like Sir* George.

Court. There she is ! If I can but disengage her from that fool Flutter—crown me, ye Schemers, with immortal wreaths.

Lady Fran. O my dear Sir George ! I rejoice to meet you—an old Conjuror has been frightening me with his Prophecies.—Where's Mrs. Rackett?

Court. In the dancing-room.—I promis'd to send you to her, Mr. Flutter.

Flut. Ah ! she wants me to dance. With all my heart.
                                                    [*Exit.*

Lady Fran. Why do you keep on your mask ?—'tis too warm.

Court. 'Tis very warm—I want air—let us go.

Lady Fran. You seem quite agitated.——Sha'n't we bid our company adieu ?

Court. No, no ;—there's no time for forms. I'll just give directions to the carriage, and be with you in a moment. (*Going, steps back.*) Put on your mask ; I have a particular reason for it.   [*Exit.*

Saville *advances with* Kitty.

Sav. Now, Kitty, you know your lesson. Lady Frances, (*takes off his mask*) let me lead you to your Husband.

Lady Fran. Heavens ! is Mr. Saville the Conjuror ? Sir George is just stept to the door to give directions.—We are going home immediately.

                         I   *Lady*

Sav. No, Madam, you are deceiv'd : Sir George is this way.

Lady Fran. This is aftonifhing !

Sav. Be not alarm'd : you have efcap'd a fnare, and fhall be in fafety in a moment.

[*Ex.* Saville *and Lady* Frances.

Enter Courtall, *and feizes* Kitty's *Hand.*

Court. Now !

Kitty. 'Tis pity to go fo foon.

Court. Perhaps I may bring you back, my Angel——but go now, you muft.   [*Exit.*]   [*Mufic.*]

Doricourt *and* Letitia *come forward.*

Dor. By Heavens ! I never was charm'd till now.——Englifh beauty—French vivacity—wit—elegance. Your name, my Angel !—tell me your name, though you perfift in concealing your face.

Let. My name has a fpell in it.

Dor. I thought fo ; it muft be *Charming.*

Let. But if reveal'd, the charm is broke.

Dor. I'll anfwer for its force.

Let. Suppofe it Harriet, or Charlotte, or Maria, or——

Dor. Hang Harriet, and Charlotte, and Maria—the name your Father gave ye !

Let. That can't be worth knowing, 'tis fo tranfient a thing.

Dor. How, tranfient ?

Let. Heav'n forbid my name fhould be *lafting* till I am married.

Dor. Married ! The chains of Matrimony are too heavy and vulgar for fuch a fpirit as yours.——The flowery wreaths of Cupid are the only bands you fhould wear.

Let. They are the lighteft, I believe : but 'tis poffible to wear thofe of Marriage gracefully.——Throw 'em loofely round, and twift 'em in a True-Lover's Knot for the Bofom.

Dor. An Angel ! But what will you be when a Wife !

Let. A Woman.—If my Hufband fhould prove a Churl, a Fool.

a Fool, or a Tyrant, I'd break his heart, ruin his fortune, elope with the firſt pretty Fellow that aſk'd me—
and return the contempt of the world with ſcorn, whilſt
my feelings prey'd upon my life.

Dor. Amazing ! [*Aſide*] What if you lov'd him, and
he were worthy of your love ?

Let. Why, then I'd be any thing—and all !—Grave,
gay, capricious — the ſoul of whim, the ſpirit of variety—live with him in the eye of faſhion, or in the
ſhade of retirement——change my country, my ſex,—
feaſt with him in an Eſquimaux hut, or a Perſian pavi-
lion—join him in the victorious war-dance on the
borders of Lake Ontario, or ſleep to the ſoft breathings
of the flute in the cinnamon groves of Ceylon—dig
with him in the mines of Golconda, or enter the dangerous precincts of the Mogul's Seraglo——cheat him
of his wiſhes, and overturn his empire to reſtore the
Huſband of my Heart to the bleſſings of Liberty and Love.

Dor. Delightful wildneſs ! Oh, to catch thee, and hold
thee for ever in this little cage ! [*Attempting to claſp her.*

Let. Hold, Sir ! Though Cupid muſt give the bait
that tempts me to the ſnare, 'tis Hymen muſt ſpread the
net to catch me.

Dor. 'Tis in vain to aſſume airs of coldneſs——Fate
has ordain'd you mine.

Let. How do you know ?

Dor. I feel it *here*. I never met with a Woman ſo perfectly to my taſte ; and I won't believe it form'd you ſo,
on purpoſe to tantalize me.

Let. This moment is worth my whole exiſtence.[*Aſide.*]

Dar. Come, ſhew me your face, and rivet my chains.

Let. To-morrow you ſhall be ſatisfied.

Dor. To-morrow ! and not to-night ?

Let. No.

Dor. Where then ſhall I wait on you to-morrow ?——
Where ſee you ?

Let.

Let. You fhall fee me in an hour when you leaft expect me.

Dor. Why all this myftery?

Let. I like to be myfterious. At prefent be content to
know that I am a Woman of Family and Fortune. Adieu!

Enter Hardy.

Har. Adieu! Then I am come at the fag end. [*Afide.*]

Dor. Let me fee you to your carriage.

Let. As you value knowing me, ftir not a ftep. If I am
follow'd, you never fee me more.   [*Exit.*

Dor. Barbarous Creature! She's gone! What, and
is this really ferious?—am I in love?——Pho! it can't
be——O Flutter! do you know that charming Creature?

Enter Flutter.

Flut. What charming Creature? I pafs'd a thoufand.

Dor. She went out at that door, as you enter'd.

Flut. Oh, yes;—I know her very well.

Dor. Do you, my dear Fellow? Who?

Flut. She's kept by Lord George Jennett.

Har. Impudent Scoundrel! [*Afide.*]

Dor. Kept!!!

Flut. Yes; Colonel Gorget had her firft;— then Mr.
Loveill;—then—I forget exactly how many; and at laft
fhe's Lord George's. [*Talks to other Mafks.*]

Dor. I'll murder Gorget, poifon Lord George, and
fhoot myfelf.

Har. Now's the time, I fee, to clear up the whole. Mr.
Doricourt!—I fay—Flutter was miftaken; I know who
you are in love with.

Dor. A ftrange *rencontre!* Who?

Har. My Letty.

Dor. Oh! I underftand your rebuke;—'tis too foon,
Sir, to affume the Father-in-law.

Har. Zounds! what do you mean by that? I tell you
that the Lady you admire, is Letitia Hardy.

Dor.

Dor. I am glad *you* are so well satisfied with the state of my heart.—I wish I was. [*Exit.*

Har. Stop a moment.—Stop, I say! What, you won't? Very well—if I don't play you a trick for this, may I never be a Grand-father! I'll plot *with* Letty now, and not against her; aye, hang me if I don't. There's something in my head, that shall tingle in his heart.—He shall have a lecture upon impatience, that I foresee he'll be the better for as long as he lives. [*Exit.*

Saville *comes forward with other Masks.*

Sav. Flutter, come with us; we're going to raise a laugh at Courtall's.

Flut. With all my heart. "Live to Live," was my Father's motto: "Live to Laugh," is mine. [*Exit.*

SCENE———Courtall's.

Enter Kitty *and* Courtall.

Kitty. Where have you brought me, Sir George? This is not our home.

Court. 'Tis *my* home, beautiful Lady Frances! [*Kneels, and takes off his Mask.*] Oh, forgive the ardency of my passion, which has compell'd me to deceive you.

Kitty. Mr. Courtall! what will become of me?

Court. Oh, say but that you pardon the Wretch who adores you. Did you but know the agonizing tortures of my heart, since I had the felicity of conversing with you this morning———or the despair that now—[*Knock.*]

Kitty. Oh! I'm undone!

Court. Zounds! my dear Lady Frances. I am not at home. Rascal! do you hear?———Let no body in; I am not at home.

Serv. [*Without*] Sir, I told the Gentlemen so.

Court. Eternal curses! they are coming up. Step into this room, adorable Creature! *one* moment; I'll throw them out of the window if they stay three.

[*Exit* Kitty; *through the back scene.*

Enter

Enter Saville, Flutter, *and Masks.*

Flut. O Gemini! beg the Petticoat's pardon.—Juſt ſaw a corner of it.

1ſt Maſk. No wonder admittance was ſo difficult. I thought you took us for Bailiffs.

Court. Upon my ſoul, I am deviliſh glad to ſee you—but you perceive now I am circumſtanc'd. Excuſe me at this moment.

2d Maſk. Tell us who 'tis then.

Court. Oh, fie!

Flut. We won't blab.

Court. I can't, upon honour.—Thus far—She's a Wo-man of the firſt Character and Rank. Saville, [*takes him aſide*] have I influence, or have I not?

Sav. Why, ſure, you do not inſinuate—

Court. No, not inſinuate, but ſwear, that ſhe's now in my bed-chamber:—by gad, I don't deceive you.—There's Generalſhip, you Rogue! Such an humble, diſtant, ſighing Fellow as thou art, at the end of a ſix-months ſiege, would have *boaſted* of a kiſs from her glove.——I only give the ſignal, and—pop!—ſhe's in my arms.

Sav. What, Lady Fran——

Court. Huſh! You ſhall ſee her name to-morrow morn-ing in red letters at the end of my liſt. Gentlemen, you muſt excuſe me now. Come and drink chocolate at twelve, but—

Sav. Aye, let us go, out of reſpect to the Lady:—'tis a Perſon of Rank.

Flut. Is it?—Then I'll have a peep at her. (*Runs to the door in the back Scene.*)

Court. This is too much, Sir. (*Trying to prevent him.*)

1ſt Maſk. By Jupiter, we'll all have a peep.

Court. Gentlemen, conſider—for Heaven's ſake—— a Lady of Quality. What will be the conſequences?

Flut. The conſequences!—Why, you'll have your throat cut, that's all—but I'll write your Elegy. So,

now

now for the door ! [*Part open the door, whilst the rest
hold* Courtall.]——Beg your Ladyship's pardon, whoever
you are : [*Leads her out.*] Emerge from darkness like
the glorious Sun, and bless the wond'ring circle with
your charms. [*Takes off her Mask.*]

Sav. Kitty Willis ! ha ! ha ! ha !

Omnes. Kitty Willis ! ha ! ha ! ha ! Kitty Willis !

1st Mask. Why, what a Fellow you are, Courtall, to
attempt imposing on your friends in this manner ! A
Lady of Quality—an Earl's Daughter—Your Ladyship's most obedient.——Ha ! ha ! ha !

Sav. Courtall, have you influence, or have you not ?

Flut. The Man's moon-struck.

Court. Hell, and ten thousand Furies, seize you all together !

Kitty. What ! me, too, Mr. Courtall ? me, whom you
have knelt to, pray'd to, and adored ?

Flut. That's right, Kitty ; give him a little more.

Court. Disappointed and laugh'd at !——

Sav. Laugh'd at and despis'd. I have fullfiled my
design, which was to expose your villainy, and laugh at
your presumption. Adieu, Sir ! Remember how you
again boast of your influence with Women of Rank ; and,
when you next want amusement, dare not to look up to
the virtuous and to the noble for a Companion.

[*Exit, leading* Kitty.

Flut. And, Courtall, before you carry a Lady into your
bed-chamber again, look under her mask, d'ye hear ?

[*Exit.*

Court. There's no bearing this ! I'll set off for Paris
directly.   [*Exit.*

END OF THE FOURTH ACT.

ACT V.

SCENE I.——*Hardy's*.

Enter Hardy *and* Villers.

Villers.

WHIMSICAL enough! Dying for her, and hates her; believes her a Fool, and a Woman of brilliant Underſtanding!

Har. As true as you are alive;—but when I went up to him laſt night, at the Pantheon, out of downright good-nature to explain things——my Gentleman whips round upon his heel, and ſnapt me as ſhort as if I had been a beggar-woman with ſix children, and he Overſeer of the Pariſh.

Vill. Here comes the Wonder-worker—[*Enter* Letitia.] Here comes the Enchantreſs, who can go to Maſquerades, and ſing and dance, and talk a Man out of his wits!—— But pray, have we Morning Maſquerades?

Let. Oh, no—but I am ſo enamour'd of this all-con-quering Habit, that I could not reſiſt putting it on, the moment I had breakfaſted. I ſhall wear it on the day I am married, and then lay it by in ſpices—like the mi-raculous Robes of St. Bridget.

Vil. That's as moſt Brides do. The charms that helped to catch the Huſband, are generally *laid by*, one after another, 'till the Lady grows a downright Wife, and then runs crying to her Mother, becauſe ſhe has trans-form'd her *Lover* into a downright Huſband.

Har. Liſten to me.—I ha'n't ſlept to-night, for think-ing of plots to plague Doricourt;—and they drove one another out of my head ſo quick, that I was as giddy as a gooſe, and could make nothing of 'em. —— I wiſh to goodneſs you could contrive ſomething.   *Vill.*

Vill. Contrive to plague him! Nothing fo eafy. Don't undeceive him, Madam, 'till he is your Hufband. Marry him whilft he poffeffes the fentiments you labour'd to give him of Mifs Hardy—and when you are his Wife——

Let. Oh, Heavens! I fee the whole—that's the very thing. My dear Mr. Villers, you are the divineft Man.

Vill. Don't make love to me, Huffey.

Enter Mrs. Racket.

Mrs. Rack. No, pray don't—for I defign to have Villers myfelf in about fix years.—There's an oddity in him that pleafes me.—He holds Women in contempt; and I fhould like to have an opportunity of breaking his heart for that.

Vill. And when I am heartily tired of life, I know no Woman whom I would with more pleafure make my Executioner.

Har. It cannot be——I forefee it will be impoffible to bring it about. You know the wedding wasn't to take place this week or more—and Letty will never be able to play the Fool fo long.

Vill. The knot fhall be tied to-night.——I have it all here, *(pointing to his forehead:)* the licence is ready. Feign yourfelf ill, fend for Doricourt, and tell him you can't go out of the world in peace, except you fee the ceremony performed.

Har. I feign myfelf ill! I could as foon feign myfelf a Roman Ambaffador.——I was never ill in my life, but with the tooth-ach—when Letty's Mother was a breeding I had all the qualms.

Vill. Oh, I have no fears for *you.*—But what fays Mifs Hardy? Are you willing to make the irrevocable vow before night?

Let. Oh, Heavens!—I—I—'Tis fo exceeding fudden, that really——

Mrs. Rack. That really fhe is frighten'd out of her wits—left it fhould be impoffible to bring matters about. But *I* have taken the fcheme into my protection, and you

K   fhall

fhall be Mrs. Doricourt before night. Come, [*to Mr. Hardy*] to bed directly : your room fhall be cramm'd with phials, and all the apparatus of Death ;——then heigh prefto ! for Doricourt.

Vill. You go and put off your conquering drefs, [*to Letty*] and get all your aukward airs ready—And you practife a few groans [*to Hardy*.]—And you—if poffible—an air of gravity [*to Mrs.* Racket]. I'll anfwer for the plot.

Let. Married in jeft ! 'Tis an odd idea ! Well, I'll venture it.   [*Ex. Letitia and Mrs.* Racket.

Vill. Aye, I'll be fworn ! [*looks at his watch*] 'tis paft three. The Budget's to be open'd this morning. I'll juft ftep down to the Houfe.——Will you go ?

Har. What ! with a mortal ficknefs ?

Vill. What a Blockhead ! I believe, if half of us were to ftay away with mortal ficknefies, it would be for the health of the Nation. Good-morning.—Ill call and feel your pulfe as I come back.   [*Exit.*

Har. You won't find 'em over brifk, I fancy. I forefee fome ill happening from this making believe to die before one's time. But hang it—a-hem !—I am a ftout man yet ; only fifty-fix—What's that ? In the laft Yearly Bill there were three lived to above an hundred. Fifty-fix !—— Fiddle-de-dee ! I am not afraid, not I.   [*Exit.*

S C E N E II.——*Doricourt's.*
Doricourt *in his Robe-de-Chambre.*

Enter Saville.

Sav. Undrefs'd fo late ?

Doric. I didn't go to bed 'till late—'twas late before I flept—late when I rofe. Do you know Lord George Jennett ?

Sav. Yes.

Doric. Has he a Miftrefs ?

Sav. Yes.

Doric. What fort of a creature is fhe ?

                                    Sav

Sav. Why, fhe fpends him three thoufand a year with
the eafe of a Duchefs, and entertains his friends with the
grace of a *Ninon.* *Ergo,* fhe is handfome, fpirited, and
clever. [Doricourt *walks about difordered.*] In the name
of Caprice, what ails you?

Doric. You have hit it—*Elle eft mon Caprice*—The Miftrefs of Lord George Jennett is my caprice—Oh, infuf-
ferable!

Sav. What, you faw her at the Mafquerade?

Doric. Saw her, *lov'd* her, *died* for her—without knowing her—And now the curfe is, I can't hate her.

Sav. Ridiculous enough! All this diftrefs about a Kept
Woman, whom any man may have, I dare fwear, in a
fortnight—They've been jarring fome time.

Doric. Have her! The fentiment I have conceived for
the Witch is fo unaccountable, that, in that line, I cannot bear her idea. Was fhe a Woman of Honour, for
a Wife, I cou'd adore her—but, I really believe, if fhe
fhould fend me an affignation, I fhould hate her.

Sav. Hey-day! This founds like Love. What becomes of poor Mifs Hardy?

Doric. Her name has given me an ague. Dear Saville,
how fhall I contrive to make old Hardy cancel the engagements! The moiety of the eftate which he will for-
feit, fhall be his the next moment, by deed of gift.

Sav. Let me fee—Can't you get it infinuated that you
are a dev'lifh wild fellow; that you are an Infidel, and
attached to wenching, gaming, and fo forth?

Doric. Aye, fuch a character might have done fome
good two centuries back.——But who the devil can it
frighten now? I believe it muft be the mad fcheme, at
laft.—There, will that do for the grin?

Sav. Ridiculous!—But, how are you certain that the
Woman who has fo bewildered you, belongs to Lord
George?

Doric. Flutter told me fo.

Sav. Then fifty to one againft the intelligence.

Doric.

Doric. It muſt be ſo. There was a myſtery in her manner, for which nothing elſe can account. ·[*A violent rap.*] Who can this be? [Saville *looks out.*]

Sav. The proverb is your anſwer—'tis Flutter himſelf. Tip him a ſcene of the Mad-man, and ſee how it takes.

Doric. I will—a good way to ſend it about town. Shall it be of the melancholy kind, or the raving?

Sav. Rant!—rant!—Here he comes.

Doric. Talk not to me who can pull comets by the beard, and overſet an iſland!

Enter Flutter.

There! This is he!—this is he who hath ſent my poor ſoul, without coat or breeches, to be toſſed about in ether like a duck-feather! Villain, give me my ſoul again!

Flut. Upon my ſoul I hav'n't got it. [*Exceedingly frightened.*]

Sav. Oh, Mr. Flutter, what a melancholy ſight!——I little thought to have ſeen my poor friend reduced to this.

Flut. Mercy defend me! What's he mad?

Sav. You ſee how it is. A curſed Italian Lady—Jea-louſy—gave him a drug; and every full of the moon——

Doric. Moon! Who dares talk of the Moon? The patroneſs of genius—the rectifier of wits—the——Oh! here ſhe is!—I feel her—ſhe tugs at my brain—ſhe has it—ſhe has it——Oh! [*Exit.*

Flut. Well! this is dreadful! exceeding dreadful, I proteſt. Have you had Monro?

Sav. Not yet. The worthy Miſs Hardy—what a misfortune!

Flut. Aye, very true.—Do they know it?

Sav. Oh, no; the paroxyſm ſeized him but this morn-ing.

Flut. Adieu! I can't ſtay. [*Going in great haſte.*]

Sav. But you muſt. (*holding him*) Stay, and aſſiſt me: —perhaps he'll return again in a moment; and, when he is in this way, his ſtrength is prodigious.

Flut. Can't indeed—can't upon my ſoul. [*Exit.*
Sav.

Sav. Flutter—Don't make a miftake, now;—remember 'tis Doricourt that's mad.   [*Exit.*

Flut. Yes—you mad.

Sav. No, no; Doricourt.

Flut. Egad, I'll fay you are both mad, and then I can't miftake.   [*Exeunt feverally.*

SCENE III.——Sir *George Touchwood's.*

Enter Sir George, *and Lady* Frances.

Sir Geo. The bird is efcaped—Courtall is gone to France.

Lady Fran. Heaven and earth! Have ye been to feek him?

Sir Geo. Seek him! Aye.

Lady Fran. How did you get his name? I fhould never have told it you.

Sir Geo. I learnt it in the firft Coffee-houfe I entered.—Every body is full of the ftory.

Lady Fran. Thank Heaven! he's gone!—But I have a ftory for you—The Hardy family are forming a plot upon your Friend Doricourt, and we are expected in the evening to affift.

Sir Geo. With all my heart, my Angel; but I can't ftay to hear it unfolded. They told me Mr. Saville would be at home in half an hour, and I am impatient to fee him. The adventure of laft night ——

Lady Fran. Think of it only with gratitude. The danger I was in has overfet a new fyftem of conduct, that, perhaps, I was too much inclined to adopt. But henceforward, my dear Sir George, you fhall be my conftant Companion, and Protector. And, when they ridicule the unfafhionable Monfters, the felicity of our hearts fhall make their fatire pointlefs.

Sir Geo. Charming Angel! You almoft reconcile me to Courtall. Hark! here's company (*ftepping to the door.*) 'Tis your lively Widow—I'll ftep down the back ftairs, to efcape her.   [*Exit Sir George.*

Enter

Enter Mrs. Racket.

Mrs. Rack. Oh, Lady Frances! I am fhock'd to death. —Have you received a card from us?

Lady Fran. Yes; within thefe twenty minutes.

Mrs. Rack. Aye, 'tis of no confequence.——'Tis all over—Doricourt is mad.

Lady Fran. Mad!

Mrs. Rack. My poor Letitia!—Juft as we were enjoying ourfelves with the profpect of a fcheme that was planned for their mutual happinefs, in came Flutter, breathlefs, with the intelligence:—I flew here to know if you had heard it.

Lady Fran. No, indeed—and I hope it is one of Mr. Flutter's dreams.

Enter Saville.

A-propos; now we fhall be informed. Mr. Saville, I rejoice to fee you, though Sir George will be difappointed: he's gone to your lodgings.

Sav. I fhould have been happy to have prevented Sir George. I hope your Ladyfhip's adventure laft night did not difturb your dreams?

Lady Fran. Not at all; for I never flept a moment. My efcape, and the importance of my obligations to you, employed my thoughts. But we have juft had fhocking intelligence—Is is true that Doricourt is mad?

Sav. So; the bufinefs is done. (*Afide.*) Madam, I am forry to fay, that I have juft been a melancholy witnefs of his ravings: he was in the height of a paroxyfm.

Mrs. Rack. Oh, there can be no doubt of it. Flutter told us the whole hiftory. Some Italian Princefs gave him a drug, in a box of fweetmeats, fent to him by her own page; and it renders him lunatic every month. Poor Mifs Hardy! I never felt fo much on any occafion in my life.

Sav. To foften your concern, I will inform you, Madam, that Mifs Hardy is lefs to be pitied than you imagine.

Mrs.

Mrs. Rack. Why fo, Sir?

Sav. 'Tis rather a delicate fubject—but he did not love Mifs Hardy.

Mrs. Rack. He did love Mifs Hardy, Sir, and would have been the happieft of men.

Sav. Pardon me, Madam; his heart was not only free from that Lady's chains, but abfolutely captivated by another.

Mrs. Rack. No, Sir—no. It was Mifs Hardy who captivated him. She met him laft night at the Mafque-rade, and charmed him in difguife—He profeffed the moft violent paffion for her; and a plan was laid, this even-ing, to cheat him into happinefs.

Sav. Ha! ha! ha!—Upon my foul, I muft beg your pardon; I have not eaten of the Italian Princefs's box of fweetmeats, fent by her own page; and yet I am as mad as Doricourt, ha! ha! ha!

Mrs. Rack. So it appears—What can all this mean?

Sav. Why, Madam, he is at prefent in his perfect fenfes; but he'll lofe 'em in ten minutes, through joy.— The madnefs was only a feint, to avoid marrying Mifs Hardy, ha! ha! ha!—I'll carry him the intelligence directly. *(Going.)*

Mrs. Rack. Not for worlds. I owe him revenge, now, for what he has made us fuffer. You muft promife not to divulge a fyllable I have told you; and when Dori-ricourt is fummoned to Mr. Hardy's, prevail on him to come—madnefs, and all.

Lady Fran. Pray do. I fhould like to fee him fhewing off, now I am in the fecret.

Sav. You muft be obeyed; though 'tis inhuman to conceal his happinefs.

Mrs. Rack. I am going home; fo I'll fet you down at his lodgings, and acquaint you, by the way, with our whole fcheme. *Allons!*

Sav. I attend you *(leading her out.)*

Mrs. Rack. You won't fail us?

              [*Ex.* Saville, *and Mrs.* Racket.

Lady Fran. No; depend on us.   [*Exit.*

SCENE IV.——*Doricourt's.*

Doricourt *seated, reading.*

Doric. (*flings away the book*) What effect can the morals of Fourscore have on a mind torn with passion?
(*musing*) Is it possible such a soul as her's, can support it-
self in so humiliating a situation? A kept Woman! (*rising*)
Well, well—I am glad it is so—I am glad it is so!

Enter Saville.

Sav. What a happy dog you are, Doricourt! I might
have been mad, or beggar'd, or pistol'd myself, without
its being mentioned—But you, forsooth! the whole Female World is concerned for. I reported the state of your
brain to five different women—The lip of the first trem-
bled; the white bosom of the second heaved a sigh; the
third ejaculated, and turned her eye—to the glass; the
fourth blessed herself; and the fifth said, whilst she pinned
a curl, "Well, now, perhaps, he'll be an amusing Com-
" panion; his native dullness was intolerable."

Doric. Envy! sheer envy, by the smiles of Hebe!——
There are not less than forty pair of the brightest eyes
in town will drop crystals, when they hear of my misfortune.

Sav. Well, but I have news for you:—Poor Hardy is
confined to his bed; they say he is going out of the
world by the first post, and he wants to give you his bles-
sing.

Doric. Ill! so ill! I am sorry from my soul. He's a
worthy little Fellow—if he had not the gift of foreseeing
so strongly.

Sav. Well; you must go and take leave.

                      Doric.

Doric. What! to act the Lunatic in the dying Man's chamber?

Sav. Exactly the thing; and will bring your bufinefs to a fhort iffue : for his laft commands muft be, That you are not to marry his Daughter.

Doric. That's true, by Jupiter !—and yet, hang it, impofe upon a poor fellow at fo ferious a moment !— I can't do it.

Sav. You muft, 'faith. I am anfwerable for your appearance, though it fhould be in a ftrait waiftcoat. He knows your fituation, and feems the more defirous of an interview.

Doric. I don't like encountering Racket.—She's an arch little devil, and will difcover the cheat.

Sav. There's a fellow !—Cheated Ninety-nine Women, and now afraid of the Hundredth.

Doric. And with reafon—for that hundredth is a Widow.　　　　　　　　　　　　　　　　[*Exeunt.*

S C E N E V.—— *Hardy's.*

Enter Mrs. Racket, *and Mifs* Ogle.

Mifs Ogle. And fo Mifs Hardy is actually to be married to-night?

Mrs. Rack. If her Fate does not deceive her. You are apprifed of the fcheme, and we hope it will fucceed.

Mifs Ogle. Deuce take her ! fhe's fix years younger than I am. (*Afide*)—Is Mr. Doricourt handfome?

Mrs. Rack. Handfome, generous, young, and rich.—— There's a Hufband for ye ! Isn't he worth pulling caps for ?

Mifs Ogle. I' my confcience, the Widow fpeaks as though fhe'd give cap, ears, and all for him. (*Afide.*) I wonder you didn't try to catch this wonderful Man, Mrs. Racket?

Mrs. Rack. Really, Mifs Ogle, I had not time. Befides, when I marry, fo many ftout young fellows will

L　　　　　　　hang

hang themfelves, that, out of regard to fociety, in thefe fad times, I fhall poftpone it for a few years. This will coft her a new lace—I heard it crack. (*Afide.*)

Enter Sir George, *and Lady* Frances.

Sir Geo. Well, here we are.—But where's the Knight of the Woeful Countenance?

Mrs. Rack. Here foon, I hope—for a woeful Night it will be without him.

Sir Geo. Oh, fie! do you condefcend to pun?

Mrs. Rack. Why not? It requires genius to make a good pun—fome men of bright parts can't reach it. I know a Lawyer who writes them on the back of his briefs; and fays they are of great ufe—in a dry caufe.

Enter Flutter.

Flut. Here they come!—Here they come!——Their coach ftopped, as mine drove off.

Lady Fran. Then Mifs Hardy's fate is at a crifis.— She plays a hazardous game, and I tremble for her.

Sav. (*without*) Come, let me guide you!—This way, my poor Friend! Why are you fo furious?

Doric. (*without*) The Houfe of Death—to the Houfe of Death!

Enter Doricourt, *and* Saville.

Ah! this is the fpot!

Lady Fran. How wild and fiery he looks!

Mifs Ogle. Now, I think, he looks terrified.

Flut. Poor creature, how his eyes work!

Mrs. Rack. I never faw a Madman before—Let me examine him—Will he bite?

Sav. Pray keep out of his reach, Ladies—You don't know your danger. He's like a Wild Cat, if a fudden thought feifes him.

Sir Geo. You talk like a Keeper of Wild Cats—How much do you demand for fhewing the Monfter?

Doric. I don't like this—I muft roufe their fenfibility. There! there fhe darts through the air in liquid flames!

Down

Down again! Now I have her——Oh, fhe burns, fhe fcorches!—Oh! fhe eats into my very heart!

Omnes. Ha! ha! ha!

Mrs. Rack. He fees the Apparition of the wicked Italian Princefs.

Flut. Keep her Highnefs faft, Doricourt.

Mifs Ogle. Give her a pinch, before you let her go.

Doric. I am laughed at!

Mrs. Rack. Laughed at—aye, to be fure; why, I could play the Madman better than you.—There! there fhe is! Now I have her! Ha! ha! ha!

Doric. I knew that Devil would difcover me. *(Afide)* I'll leave the houfe:——I'm covered with confufion. *(Going.)*

Sir Geo. Stay, Sir—You muft not go. 'Twas poorly done, Mr. Doricourt, to affect madnefs, rather than fulfil your engagements.

Doric. Affect madnefs!—Saville, what can I do?

Sav. Since you are difcovered, confefs the whole.

Mifs Ogle. Aye, turn Evidence, and fave Yourfelf.

Doric. Yes; fince my defigns have been fo unaccountably difcovered, I will avow the whole. I cannot love Mifs Hardy—and I will never ———

Sav. Hold, my dear Doricourt! be not fo rafh. What will the world fay to fuch ———

Doric. Damn the world! What will the world give me for the lofs of happinefs? Muft I facrifice my peace, to pleafe the world?

Sir Geo. Yes, every thing, rather than be branded with difhonour.

Lady Fran. Though *our* arguments fhould fail, there *is* a Pleader, whom you furely cannot withftand—the dying Mr. Hardy fupplicates you not to forfake his Child.

Enter Villers.

Vill. Mr. Hardy requefts you to grant him a moment's

con-

converfation, Mr. Doricourt, though you fhould perfift to fend him miferable to the grave. Let me conduct you to his chamber.

Doric. Oh, aye, any where ; to the Antipodes—to the Moon—Carry me—Do with me what you will.

Mrs. Rack Mortification and difappointment, then, are fpecifics in a cafe of ftubbornnefs.—I'll follow, and let you know what paffes.

[*Exeunt* Villers, Doricourt, *Mrs.* Racket, *and Mifs* Ogle.

Flut. Ladies, Ladies, have the charity to take me with you, that I may make no blunder in repeating the ftory. [*Exit* Flutter.

Lady Fran. Sir George, you don't know Mr. Saville.
[*Exit Lady* Frances.

Sir Geo. Ten thoufand pardons—but I will not pardon myfelf, for not obferving you. I have been with the ut-moft impatience at your door twice to-day.

Sav. I am concerned you had fo much trouble, Sir George.

Sir Geo. Trouble! what a word !—I hardly know how to addrefs you ; I am diftreffed beyond meafure ; and it is the higheft proof of my opinion of your honour, and the delicacy of your mind, that I open my heart to you.

Sav. What has difturbed you, Sir George ?

Sir Geo. Your having preferved Lady Frances, in fo imminent a danger. Start not, Saville ; to protect Lady Frances, was my right. You have wrefted from me my deareft privilege.

Sav. I hardly know how to anfwer fuch a reproach. I cannot apologize for what I have done.

Sir Geo. I do not mean to reproach you ; I hardly know what I mean. There is one method by which you may reftore peace to me ; I cannot endure that my Wife fhould be fo infinitely indebted to any man who is lefs than my Brother.

Sav.

Sav. Pray explain yourfelf.

Sir Geo. I have a Sifter, Saville, who is amiable; and you are worthy of her. I fhall give her a commiffion to fteal your heart, out of revenge for wHat you have done.

Sav. I am infinitely honoured, Sir George; but ——

Sir Geo. I cannot liften to a fentence which begins with fo unpromifing a word. You muft go with us into Hampfhire; and, if you fee each other with the eyes I do, your felicity will be complete. I know no one, to whofe heart I would fo readily commit the care of my Sifter's happinefs.

Sav. I will attend you to Hampfhire, with pleafure; but not on the plan of retirement. Society has claims on Lady Frances, that forbid it.

Sir Geo. Claims, Saville !

Sav. Yes, claims; Lady Frances was born to be the ornament of Courts. She is fufficiently alarmed, not to wander beyond the reach of her Protector;—and, from the Britifh Court, the moft tenderly-anxious Hufband could not wifh to banifh his Wife. Bid her keep in her eye the bright Example who prefides there; the fplendour of whofe rank yields to the fuperior luftre of her Virtue.

Sir Geo. I allow the force of your argument. Now for intelligence !

  Enter *Mrs.* Racket, *Lady* Frances, *and* Flutter.]

Mrs. Rack. Oh ! Heav'ns ! do you know ——

Flut. Let me tell the ftory——As foon as Doricourt —

Mrs. Rack. I proteft you fha'n't—faid Mr. Hardy ——

Flut. No, 'twas Doricourt fpoke firft—fays he—No, 'twas the Parfon—fays he ——

Mrs. Rack. Stop his mouth, Sir George—he'll fpoil the tale.

Sir Geo. Never heed circumftances—the refult—the refult.

Mrs. Rack. No, no; you fhall have it in form.—Mr. Hardy performed the Sick Man like an Angel—He fat

up

up in his bed, and talked fo pathetically, that the tears ftood in Doricourt's eyes.

Flut. Aye, ftood—they did not drop, but ftood.—I fhall, in future, be very exact. The Parfon feized the moment; you know, they never mifs an opportunity.

Mrs. Rack. Make hafte, faid Doricourt; if I have time to reflect, poor Hardy will die unhappy.

Flut. They were got as far as the Day of Judgement, when we flipt out of the room.

Sir Geo. Then, by this time, they muft have reached *Amazement*, which, every body knows, is the end of Matrimony.

Mrs. Rack. Aye, the Reverend Fathers ended the fervice with that word, Prophetically——to teach the Bride what a capricious Monfter a Hufband is.

Sir Geo. I rather think it was Sarcaftically—to prepare the Bridegroom for the unreafonable humours and vagaries of his Help-mate.

Lady Fran. Here comes the Bridegroom of to-night.

Enter Doricourt *and* Villers.—Villers *whifpers* Saville, *who goes out.*

Omnes. Joy! joy! joy!

Mifs Ogle. If *he's* a fample of Bridegrooms, keep me fingle!—A younger Brother, from the Funeral of his Father, could not carry a more fretful countenance.

Flut. Oh!—Now, he's melancholy mad, I fuppofe.

Lady Fran. You do not confider the importance of the occafion.

Vill. No; nor how fhocking a thing it is for a Man to be forced to marry one Woman, whilft his heart is devoted to another.

Mrs. Rack. Well, now 'tis over, I confefs to you, Mr. Doricourt, I think 'twas a moft ridiculous piece of Quixotifm, to give up the happinefs of a whole life to a Man who perhaps has but a few moments to be fenfible of the facrifice.

Flut.

Flut. So it appeared to me.—But, thought I, Mr. Doricourt has travelled—he knows beft.

Doric. Zounds! Confufion!—Did ye not all fet upon me?—Didn't ye talk to me of Honour—Compaffion—Juftice?

Sir Geo. Very true—You have acted according to their dictates, and I hope the utmoft felicity of the Married State will reward you.

Doric. Never, Sir George! To Felicity I bid adieu—but I will endeavour to be content. Where is my—I muft fpeak it—where is my *Wife?*

Enter Letitia, *mafked,* led by Saville.

Sav. Mr. Doricourt, this Lady was preffing to be introduced to you.

Dor. Oh! *(Starting).*

Let. I told you laft night, you fhou'd fee me at a time when you leaft expected me—and I have kept my promife.

Vill. Whoever you are, Madam, you could not have arrived at a happier moment.—Mr. Doricourt is juft married.

Let. Married! Impoffible! 'Tis but a few hours fince he fwore to me eternal Love: I believ'd him, gave him up my Virgin heart—and now!—Ungrateful Sex!

Dor. Your Virgin heart! No, Lady——my fate, thank Heaven! yet wants that torture. Nothing but the conviction that you was another's, could have made me think one moment of Marriage, to have faved the lives of half Mankind. But this vifit, Madam, is as barbarous as unexpected. It is now my duty to forget you, which, fpite of your fituation, I found difficult enough.

Let. My fituation!—What fituation?

Dor. I muft apologife for explaining it in this company —but, Madam, I am not ignorant, that you are the companion of Lord George Jennet—and this is the only circumftance that can give me peace.

Let. I—a Companion! Ridiculous pretence! No, Sir,

know

know, to your confufion, that my heart, my honour, my
name is unfpotted as her's you have married ; my birth
equal to your own, my fortune large—That, and my perfon, might have been your's.—But, Sir, farewell! *(Going.)*

Dor. Oh, ftay a moment——Rafcal ! is fhe not ——

Flut. Who, fhe ? O Lard ! no—'Twas quite a different
perfon that I meant.—I never faw that Lady before.

Dor. Then, never fhalt thou fee her more. [*Shakes*
Flutter.]

Mrs. Rack. Have mercy upon the poor Man !—Heavens ! He'll murder him.

Dor. Murder him ! Yes, you, myfelf, and all Mankind. Sir George—Saville—Villers—'twas you who
pufh'd me on this precipice ;—'tis you who have fnatch'd
from me joy, felicity, and life.

Mrs. Rack. There ! Now, how well he acts the Madman !—This is fomething like ! I knew he would do it
well enough, when the time came.

Dor. Hard-hearted Woman ! enjoy my ruin—riot in
my wretchednefs. [Hardy *burfts in.*]

Har. This is too much. You are now the Hufband of
my Daughter; and how dare you fhew all this paffion
about another Woman ?

Dor. Alive again !

Har. Alive! aye, and merry. Here, wipe off the flour
from my face. I was never in better health and fpirits in
my life.—I forefaw t'would do—.Why, my illnefs was
only a fetch, Man ! to make you marry Letty.

Dor. It was! Bafe and ungenerous ! Well, Sir, you
fhall be gratified. The poffeffion of my heart was no object either with You, or your Daughter. My fortune and
name was all you defired, and thefe—I leave ye. My
native England I fhall quit, nor ever behold you more.
But, Lady, that in my exile I may have one confolation,
grant me the favour you denied laft night ;—let me behold

all

all that mafk conceals, that your whole image may be im-
prefs'd on my heart, and chear my diftant folitary hours.

Let. 'This is the moft awful moment of my life.   Oh,
Doricourt, the flight action of taking off my Mafk, ftamps
me the moft bleft or miferable of Women !

Dor. What can this mean ?   Reveal your face, I con-
jure you.

Let. Behold it.

Dor. Rapture ! Tranfport ! Heaven !

Flut. Now for a touch of the happy Madman.

Vill. This fcheme was mine.

Let. I will not allow that.   This little ftratagem arofe
from my difappointment, in not having made the impref-
fion on you I wifh'd.   The timidity of the Englifh character threw a veil over me, you could not penetrate.
You have forced me to emerge in fome meafure from my
natural referve, and to throw off the veil that hid me.

Dor. I am yet in a ftate of intoxication—I cannot anfwer you.—Speak on, fweet Angel !

Let. You fee I *can* be any thing ; chufe then my character—your Tafte fhall fix it.   Shall I be an *Englifh*
Wife ?—or, breaking from the bonds of Nature and Education, ftep forth to the world in all the captivating
glare of Foreign Manners ?

Dor. You fhall be nothing but yourfelf—nothing can
be captivating that you are not.   I will not wrong your
penetration, by pretending that you won my heart at the
firft interview ; but you have now my whole foul—your
perfon, your face, your mind, I would not exchange for
thofe of any other Woman breathing.

Har. A Dog ! how well he makes up for paft flights !
Coufin Racket, I wifh you a good Hufband with all
my heart.   Mr. Flutter, I'll believe every word you fay
this fortnight.   Mr. Villers, you and I have manag'd

this to a T. I never was fo merry in my life—'Gad, I believe I can dance. (*Footing.*)

Doric. Charming, charming creature !

Letit. Congratulate me, my dear friends ! Can you conceive my happinefs ?

Har. No, congratulate me ; for mine is the greateft.

Flut. No, congratulate me, that I have efcaped with life, and give me fome fticking plafter—this wild cat has torn the fkin from my throat.

Sir Geo. I expect to be among the firft who are con-gratulated—for I have recovered one Angel, while Dori-court has gained another.

Har. Pho ! pho ! Don't talk of Angels, we fhall be happier by half as Mortals. Come into the next room ; I have order'd out every drop of my Forty-eight, and I'll invite the whole parifh of St. George's, but what we'll drink it out—except one dozen, which I fhall keep under three double locks, for a certain Chriftening, that I fore-fee will happen within this twelvemonth.

Dor. My charming Bride ! It was a ftrange perver-fion of Tafte, that led me to confider the delicate timidity of your deportment, as the mark of an uninform'd mind, or inelegant manners. I feel now it is to that innate modefty, *Englifb* Hufbands owe a felicity the Married Men of other nations are ftrangers to : it is a facred veil to your own charms ; it is the fureft bulwark to your Hufband's honour ; and curfed be the hour—fhould it ever arrive— in which *Britifh* Ladies fhall facrifice to *foreign Graces* the Grace of Modefty !

F I N I S.

EPILOGUE.

*N*AY, *ceaſe, and hear me—I am come to ſcold—*
　　Whence this night's plaudits, to a thought ſo old?
To gain a Lover, hid behind a Maſk!
What's new in that? or where's the mighty taſk?
For inſtance, now—What Lady Bab, or Grace,
E'er won a Lover—in her natural Face?
Miſtake me not—French red, or blanching creams,
I ſtoop not to—for thoſe are hackney'd themes;
The arts I mean, are harder to detect,
Eaſier put on, and worn to more effect;—
As thus ————
Do Pride and Envy, with their horrid lines,
Deſtroy th' effect of Nature's ſweet deſigns?
The Maſk of Softneſs is at once applied,
And gentleſt manners ornament the Bride.

　　Do thoughts too free inform the Veſtal's eye,
Or point the glance, or warm the ſtruggling ſigh?
Not Dian's brows more rigid looks diſcloſe;
And Virtue's bluſh appears, where Paſſion glows.

　　And you, my gentle Sirs, wear Vizors too;
But here I'll ſtrip you, and expoſe to view
Your hidden features ———*Firſt I point at you.*
That well-ſtuff'd waiſtcoat, and that ruddy cheek;
That ample forehead, and that ſkin ſo ſleek,
Point out good-nature, and a gen'rous heart ——
Tyrant! ſtand forth, and, conſcious, own thy part:
Thy Wife, thy Children, tremble in thy eye;
And Peace is baniſh'd—when the Father's nigh.

Sure

Sure 'tis enchantment! See, from ev'ry side
The Masks fall off!—In charity I hide
The monstrous features rushing to my view——
Fear not, there, Grand-Papa—nor you—nor you:
For should I shew your features to each other,
Not one amongst ye'd know his Friend, or Brother.
'Tis plain, then, all the world, from Youth to Age,
Appear in Masks—Here, only, on the Stage,
You see us as we are: Here trust your eyes;
Our wish to please, admits of no disguise.

E R R A T A.

Page 53. For *badinage*, read *badiner*.
Page 59. For *my*, read *a* whole existence.

Of the Publisher may be had,

By the same AUTHOR,

THE RUNAWAY, a Comedy.
ALBINA, a Tragedy.
WHO'S THE DUPE? a Farce.
THE MAID OF ARRAGON, a Poem, Part I.

** The whole of Mrs. COWLEY's *Dramatic Works, that*
have been published, may be had in One Volume, Price 6d.
in boards, 6s. 6d. bound.

www.ingramcontent.com/pod-product-compliance
Lightning Source LLC
Chambersburg PA
CBHW020047030726
47499CB00007B/2620